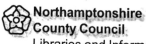

Other titles by Michael Coleman

Black Apples
Going Straight
The Snog Log
Weirdo's War

Super Crunchies
Angels FC series

ORCHARD BOOKS
96 Leonard Street, London EC2A 4XD
Orchard Books Australia
32/45-51 Huntley Street, Alexandria, NSW 2015
ISBN 1 84362 182 7
First published in Great Britain in 1998
First paperback publication in 1999
This edition first published in 2003
Text © Michael Coleman 1998
The right of Michael Coleman to be identified as the author
of this work has been asserted by him in accordance with the
Copyright, Designs and Patents Act, 1988.
A CIP catalogue record for this book is available from the British Library.
1 3 5 7 9 10 8 6 4 2
Printed in Great Britain

Michael Coleman

ORCHARD BOOKS

For Janice Goldie

A friend loveth for all times.

The Book of Proverbs, 17:17

Chapter One

'I d-don't know where to b-b-begin.'

I stutter the sentence out. I'm always at my worst when I'm feeling under pressure.

'Simple, Pete,' says Shiner softly, just like a social worker. 'Begin at the beginning.'

He's sitting opposite me. All I can hope is that now he really wants to understand if he can.

So, here goes. I'm going to tell him my story.

Well, mine and Motto's story really, but then Shiner knows that. He also knows better than anybody why Motto can't give his side of things. He arrived just after the accident happened, after all. Like me, he saw the terrible sight with his own eyes.

As for telling Shiner the basics about me, that's not necessary.

He knows my name's Peter Ellis; 'Pete' to most, 'P-P-Pete' to a cruel few, and 'Peter' to just about nobody except my mum.

He knows that Motto and I are – were – best friends.

What I'm not sure he knows, what I've got to make him believe, is that I'm innocent. What happened to Motto wasn't my fault.

So, although it isn't going to be easy, I'm going to tell him the whole story. He deserves to know the truth.

*More than that. He **needs** to know the truth.*

'OK,' I say. 'Fr-from the b-beginning...'

It seemed to me that I'd known Motto since time began. I mean, what's your earliest memory? For some kids it's playing football with their dad, or watching their mum carry in a birthday cake with a blazing candle or two.

My first memory was of Motto.

We lived in parallel roads, so that our gardens backed on to each other. That's not to say our families were equally well off. You know how it can sometimes be raining on one side of the street but not on the other? Well, our area was a bit like that. Motto's street was a good few notches up on ours. Down at the back fence, though, you really couldn't tell.

Anyway, one day we must have both toddled down to the bottom of our gardens at the same time. That's it, that's the memory: of me and Motto burbling to each other through the slats of a rickety wooden fence, like a prisoner talking to his visitor.

From then on, we just grew up together. The fence fell down and we built a den from the debris. After that we spent most days playing in there. If you added it up, the two of us probably saw more of each other than we did of the rest of the world put together.

Nothing changed when we started school. If anything, we saw more of each other than ever. After a day spent in

8

the same class it was back to the den in the evening, playing games, taking it in turns to be fugitives hiding from the police – or, more likely, Motto's sister Lorna.

'You won't go over to her side?' Motto would plead if Lorna should try to talk me into joining whatever game she had going. Even at that age the pair of them acted as though they couldn't stick each other.

'Never,' I'd say. 'I'm your friend, aren't I?'

'Cross your heart and hope to die?' He'd make the action, crossing his heart and ending with a dramatic slit across the throat.

I'd laugh and promise, 'Cross my heart and hope to die.'

Deep down, I'd have been happy for Lorna to join in with us. I didn't have either a brother or sister, and I couldn't understand why Motto should want to hide from his. Maybe if they had their time again...

Anyway, what I'm saying is that I can't remember a time when Motto and I weren't friends. Or, for that matter, when Motto wasn't surrounded by friends. Well – that's what it looked like. Whenever I saw a huddle of kids in the playground or outside the school gates you could bet that there in the middle would be Motto.

He had an endless supply of methods for turning himself into the centre of attention. If he wasn't offering to lend his latest comic to anybody who was interested, he was unwrapping something wild like a dead frog from a plastic bag.

One day I saw him wielding a huge conker I knew he'd

picked up from the tree in his garden. But Motto never let facts like that get in the way.

'Look at it!' he was yelling at the top of his voice. 'Four thousand and seventy-niner this one is! Comes from the self-same tree in Sherwood Forest what Robin Hood used when he jumped out on the Sheriff of Nottingham!'

He'd always gather a crowd without fail on the first day of the spring term, when he'd go through the little jokes he'd saved from every Christmas cracker that had been cracked in his vicinity.

'Who do boy ghosts go to the pictures with? Their ghoul-friends of course!'

'Why do RSPCA inspectors go to chip shops? To investigate cases of fish-battering!'

'How does a sailor know when he's unhappy? He gets a sinking feeling!'

Terrible, huh? After a while, though, when everybody had heard the jokes, or a little probing had revealed that Motto's conker couldn't be a Sherwood Forest special because he hadn't a clue where Nottingham was, or somebody turned up with a live hamster to outshine his dead frog, the crowd would drift away.

Then he'd spot me somewhere on the fringe. He'd come over, put his arm round my shoulders and off we'd go, best friends.

'Hey, Pete! What shall we play tonight? How about a game of war? We can pretend we're fighter pilots and Lorna's an enemy aircraft...'

10

Imagination: that's what Motto had. That's what worked the magic and put him at the centre of things – at least until the magic wore off and everybody except me drifted away.

Inventing games was another Motto tactic. Every few weeks he'd come up with something new that we'd all flock round to join in. It was only when it got under way that we'd realise that a Motto game meant a game with Motto at the centre. Games like 'Androids'.

'This is the way it works, right?' I can see him now, his eyes picking out each of us in turn as he explained. 'You are all androids.'

He rolled the word round his tongue, making it sound something that every kid should want to be. Even when he explained that an android was a robot in human form he still made it seem attractive. Then he got to the nub of the game.

'I am Zygal, Commander of all Androids. I call you Droids, for short. You have to obey my orders without question!'

Obeying an order scored points – orders like, 'Carry my bag all the way home. Shove a soggy newspaper in that postbox. Knock on that door and run for it.' Top point-scorer became Droid of the Week.

Looking back, it seems crazy. But it was imaginative and I loved it. That's what led to the shop-lifting episode.

It was Friday and we were on the way home. I was three points off the lead for Droid of the Week. Score now, I figured, and I couldn't be caught.

'How many points for buying you an ice cream,

Commander?' I asked as we reached the shops.

He wouldn't be drawn. 'I will make my decision when I see the evidence,' he said.

I dived into the shop, thinking in my hopeful way that I'd be able to talk him into making it a four-pointer. Then I saw the autograph book.

It was red, with a gold-blocked title, and sitting on a shelf within touching distance. A four-pointer if ever there was one – if I'd had enough money to buy it. I looked across the small shop. At the counter the only shop assistant on duty was busy serving somebody else. My hand snaked out and back. Oh, I knew taking it was wrong. I'm not that stupid. But in spite of that, inside my jacket it went.

I'll never forget Motto's face when I gave him that autograph book and said, 'How many points for nicking something, then?' There I was expecting a grin of congratulation and what I got was a look of disgust.

'You what? You nicked it?'

'Just now.'

He slapped it back into my hands. The game had gone too far, and he was angry that I'd spoiled it.

'Five points,' he snapped. 'I proclaim you Droid of the Week. Now take it back.'

'Take it back?'

'Yes! Stealing's wrong, don't you know that?' There was genuine panic in his voice as he insisted, 'I mean it. Take it back!'

So, while he watched from a distance to make sure I was

doing what he'd told me, I had to hang around until the assistant was busy again before I could dive into the shop and put that autograph book back where I'd found it.

On our way home the only thing he said was, 'My dad's always saying you get locked up for stealing.'

And we never played Androids again.

He must have told his parents about what happened though. The next day, Saturday, I called for him. Lorna answered the door, inviting me into the hallway while she went into the lounge to fetch Motto. She left the door open, so I overheard what was said.

'It's Pete, from over the back. He wants to know if Mark can go out.'

I heard a sudden squeak, as if somebody had levered themselves quickly up from a leather armchair.

'That little toe-rag's here, is he? Right...'

Another squeak, followed by a woman's voice, slightly fearful. 'No, don't...'

'Give me one good reason why not.'

'He took it back, Dad.' It was Motto, pleading for me. 'I made him. So he's not a thief.'

The lounge door swung open and Motto's dad stalked out. What Motto had said must have helped, though. His dad didn't bawl me out at length. Instead he concentrated on looking as frightening as he could. I knew he was tall, from the times I'd seen him before, but now he looked huge. Towering above me, braces slipped off the shoulders of his blue shirt and dangling over his trousers, he stood and glared down at me until I mumbled, 'Sorry,' because I didn't know what else to do.

His reply was short and to the point. 'If I ever hear that you've so much as thought about nicking anything, I'll be round your house like a shot. Got that?'

I didn't have time to answer. He marched off up the stairs, his heavy shoes thumping on the carpet.

From inside the lounge I heard Motto ask, 'Can I go out to play with Pete, Mum?'

She gave a sigh of resignation. 'I suppose so. But...'

Motto's mum lowered her voice as she spoke to him, but not enough. I heard what she said quite clearly. 'Mark, listen to me. Pete's a nice friend but he's a bit – well, not very clever. Not as clever as you. Understand?'

'I think so.'

'What I mean is, he looks up to you. He'll do anything you say. So – well, just remember that.'

Shiner's been nodding most of the time I've been talking, as if my being a shoplifter and Motto being the honest one was no more than he expected. Now, though, he looks a bit embarrassed.

'You remember her saying that?' He's still talking gently, mind.

I shrug. I don't see why it should bother him. She hadn't said anything I didn't know.

'How old were you then?'

'Nine.'

'Nine? Then it must have been around the time your father was—'

He stops abruptly. Maybe it's because, after what's happened to Motto, he doesn't want to use the word.

So I say it for him. It's a struggle, because it's one of the words that really gets my stutter going.

'K-k-killed? Yes.'

Chapter Two

Dad drove a crackling, spitting tube train on a route which dived from the open air of Essex into pitch black beneath the City before coming up again to clatter on to leafy places like Richmond. There, after a break, he'd climb into the cab of another train and drive all the way back again.

Same thing, day after day – until the day he didn't make it.

He'd been on the final stretch towards Upminster, where the main line between Fenchurch Street and Southend runs alongside the electrified lines. Approaching an old brick tunnel, he'd spotted a pile of masonry on the main line. Some of the stonework up at the top had collapsed; either that or it had been done deliberately – they never found out which.

Anyhow, it seemed that Dad hadn't thought twice. Driving that route so often, he'd known there was a fast train due down the main line any minute. He'd stopped and run across to try to drag the brickwork off the tracks. And he'd almost managed it. The train hit him just as he was pulling the last chunk away.

He must have heard it coming. He could have jumped, saved himself, I'm sure he could. But he hadn't. He'd hung on to move that final bit.

It made the papers, of course. They called him a hero and a picture of him in his driver's uniform appeared on most of the front pages for a few days.

I cut one out and was glad I did. A week later he'd been buried and somebody else's photograph was on the front pages. All around me life was still going on, just as it had before. That newspaper picture kept me sane.

'He's not coming back, love,' Mum had said, a month or so later. I was sitting on the floor, just gazing at it.

She didn't understand, you see. I knew he wasn't coming back. I wasn't that gormless. I needed that picture for another reason. It took me longer than usual to explain why.

'I d-don't want to f-forget what he l-looked l-like.'

Maybe it's my memory playing tricks but, until then, I don't ever remember having a stutter.

It's one thing I'll always be grateful to Motto for. He never made fun of my problem. Well – not until...but I'm jumping ahead.

At that time, he didn't. Kids can be cruel and a lot of them were.

'Here comes P-P-Pete! Want to p-p-play, P-P-Pete?'

Motto would tell them to pack it in and, if he was having one of his good spells as the centre of attraction, they'd do what he said.

Our den was still going strong but now, with Dad gone, we had unrestricted use of what had until then been a special treat. His train layout.

Mum would give him a hard time, but with a smile in her voice. 'Driving a train isn't enough for the man. He's got to play with them when he gets home as well!'

On frosty mornings she was less amused at having to chip the ice off our old car, though. Too big to fit in the house and too difficult to work on in the attic, the layout took up all the available space in the garage.

That's because I'm not talking about a little oval of track with a clockwork train. Dad's set-up, laid out on trestle boards at chest height, had the lot. Longbridge Station itself, all glass front and open concourse. Eight platforms, two for main-line trains and six for tube trains of the District and Metropolitan lines. And, sprawling out from there, in a complete out-and-back system, all you could see if you went out to look at the real thing: sidings, marshalling yards, signal boxes, bridges, tunnels, cuttings…

Motto loved it. 'Pete! This is brilliant! Invite the kids at school round! We could have a train each, fix our own timetables…'

His imagination had already been moving into overdrive, but I'd stopped him. That once, I'd stopped him.

'No. Just me and you. N-nobody else.'

'But why?'

Why? I knew why, but I wasn't sure I could explain it. I just knew that the layout was the one real part of himself that Dad had left behind.

Everywhere I looked, he was in that garage. I could see him drawing sketches and detailed diagrams. I could see him poring over them as he brought them to life, cutting wood, glueing, sticking, painting.

I could see him, hear his slow speech – the same slow way of talking I've got that makes people think I'm dumber than I really am – as he announced to his enthralled audience of one:

'Peter Ellis, my Lords, Ladies and Gentlemen, I hereby declare this model of Longbridge Station terminus...open!'

Of course, he didn't stop there. He added trains, more track, more buildings and figures. But as I grew older, I was allowed to help. OK, so 'help' isn't the right word – I was allowed to think I was helping.

'A dab of paint there, Peter. Beautiful! Couldn't have done better myself!'

Or, 'Come on, Peter. Press this switch and that train on the down line will start moving. There you go! You did that!'

They were tiny things, I know that now. But at the time I didn't. All I knew was that whenever I was in that garage with him, he made me feel like a king.

That's why I couldn't bear the thought of anybody other than Motto touching that layout. That's why, when he talked about inviting the world in to play with it, I resisted him.

'It was Dad's,' I said. 'I don't want it b-broken.'

He seemed to understand. 'You miss him, don't you?'

I remember nodding, trying not to cry. Then, as Motto said something to me, I couldn't hold off any longer and I burst into tears.

After that, though, things were different. I still thought about Dad a lot, of course. I even pinned that newspaper photograph of him on the notice board in the garage. But I'm pretty sure that was the last time I cried about him. I got angry, yes – but I didn't cry again.

You see, in my simple way, I thought I'd found a replacement. Dad had always had the knack of making me feel important. Motto, whether he knew it or not, had the same knack.

When the crowds were round him I was just one of them, on the fringes. But when they went – as they always seemed to after a while – then Motto would come looking for me.

At those moments it was as if Dad was alive again.

'He reminded you of your dad?' says Shiner. 'Is that what you're saying? A young boy reminded you of your dad?'

Put like that it sounds stupid, I know. I'm not saying that Motto acted grown up, or anything like that. Mum was there for all that stuff.

What I'm saying is that he, out of all the kids around, seemed to have an idea what it was like.

'He l-liked me,' I say simply.

It was more than that, though I can't bring myself to tell Shiner all the details. Maybe later, but not right now. I can't bring myself to tell him what Motto had said which had reduced me to tears that time.

He'd said: 'You can have my dad, Pete. Any time you want.'

I thought he'd been making the wild and generous offer of

21

a nine-year-old, as if fathers were comics you could borrow for a while.

It was only as the years passed that I came to understand what he'd really meant.

Chapter Three

Over that time, Mum and I had got our act together. As a train driver, Dad hadn't earned much. Strange, isn't it, how people like him, responsible for the safety of thousands every day, rarely do make a lot, while bankers and stockbrokers always make a packet?

Anyway – I don't know the details – there was a lump of compensation money and a bit of a widow's pension. What with that, and Mum's part-time job in the corner post office, we managed for a while. But by the time I was in my second year at Longbridge Comprehensive money was tighter than I'd realised.

'I'm going to have to get another job,' she'd said to me one evening.

'Why? C-can't you get some handout or other?'

'No, Peter,' said Mum abruptly. 'We don't qualify.'

I was inexplicably angry. 'Why not! They reckoned Dad was a hero, didn't they! It's not right!'

Right or not, Mum went out and got a second job with a contract cleaning firm. Offices don't want cleaners cleaning during the day, of course, so it meant she was in and out at all hours. I got my own front-door key and came home to an empty house most days.

Well, almost empty. Mum might not be there, but one of her jokey notes would be. However short of time she was, she'd always find time to scribble one to me.

'Peter Ellis – eat something else instead of those disgusting beefburger and gherkin concoctions you've been frying yourself all week! There's a casserole in the oven.'

'Peter Ellis, how come the clean school shirts are disappearing from the airing cupboard but I don't see any dirty ones in the wash? It couldn't by any chance be because they're growing mould in some festering corner of that tip you call a room, could it? Send out a search party, boy. Today!'

What surprised me a bit was that Motto should also turn up at school one day with a front-door key of his own. I'd known that his dad worked all hours – that had been obvious from the earliest days – but what I hadn't realised was that his mum was rarely at home either.

I found out why on the only occasion I saw him use that key. It was the day he first waved it around. I think he wanted to show it off, so instead of going to my house after school we went to his. We were half the street away from his place when we first heard the thump-thump sounds.

Motto cursed. 'Nuts. Lorna's there…and with the rest of the coven,' he added as we reached the front gate and saw the huddle of shapes through the lounge window, all jigging to the pounding music.

As he let us in with his new key, Lorna came out of the lounge. She scowled a welcome at her brother. 'You don't think you're coming in here, I hope? You and your p-p-pal.'

'And be turned into a couple of frogs?' retorted Motto with a forced grin. 'Not likely.'

We'd gone into the kitchen, where Motto raided the fridge, and were just heading upstairs, when the front door slammed open. From the landing I saw the collision as Lorna came face to face with her mother.

'Lorna! What the hell do you think you're doing?'

Motto's sister coloured. 'I...you said you wouldn't be home till late...'

'So while my back's turned you decide to have a party, do you?'

'It's not a party. We're just playing music...'

'Just playing music! The whole street can hear you're just playing music! Turn that thing off!'

By now the lounge door was wide open. Inside, the music was abruptly turned off by somebody. In the sudden calm, Lorna's half-whisper sounded clear and pathetic.

'I didn't think you'd mind...'

She was hardly given time to get the words out. Blazing with fury, not noticing us standing up at the top of the stairs, their mother waded in.

'You didn't think I'd mind!' she shouted. 'You decide to fill my house with half the toe-rags in Longbridge and you didn't think I'd mind! Of course I damn well mind!'

'They're not toe-rags,' said Lorna angrily. 'They're my friends.'

'They are in my house! Not your house! *My* house!'

Lorna snapped. Her knuckles white as she clenched her fists, she screamed, 'Well if you're so proud of *your* house, how come you're never here!'

For a moment, mother looked at daughter in stunned silence. Then she drew back her hand and slapped Lorna across the face.

I glanced at Motto, half expecting him to go downstairs and help smooth things out. Instead he simply shrugged, opened his bedroom door, and went inside.

At the bottom of the stairs Lorna was sobbing, her face buried in her hands. Her friends were pouring out of the lounge and down the path. Some of them cast sympathetic looks her way, some tried not to laugh, but most of them didn't look her way at all.

When they'd gone, Lorna got a tongue-lashing.

'How dare you criticise us! Your father has a responsible job as you well know. And I don't spend my time swanning around. I spend it helping others!'

'You think I don't know that!' Lorna jerked her head up, still crying. 'I'd do better to join them!'

'What do you mean?'

'I mean I'd see more of you if I bought my clothes at a charity shop, or ran away from home and turned up every night for a bowl of soup at the Drop-in Centre...'

'Don't you dare mock my work!' Lorna flinched as her mother raised her hand again. 'You and Mark don't know how lucky you are. You've both got a lot more to be grateful for than the people I meet every day – and those your father meets every day I shouldn't be surprised. So you shouldn't complain if in return you've got to look after yourselves sometimes…'

'Sometimes!'

'Yes, sometimes! God, to hear you talk you'd think we were never here…'

She didn't continue. It was as if she'd decided she was talking to herself. With a sudden, snapped, 'Get out of my sight,' Lorna's mother stomped off.

At the bottom of the stairs I saw why. As she slowly got to her feet, Lorna's eyes looked like diamonds set in a face of stone. She dabbed at them briefly, then pounded fiercely up the stairs. It was only when she reached the landing and almost ran into me that she had any idea that I'd seen everything.

'What are you gawping at?' she snapped.

'S-sorry,' I said.

'What?'

'I'm s-sorry. About what happened.'

Lorna looked hard at me, her eyes searching my face. I wondered if she thought I was trying to be funny.

'Don't be,' she said, her voice cold. 'I'm not.'

From behind Motto's door came a shout. 'Pete! You coming in or what? Leave the squawk-box to herself.'

Lorna looked for a moment as if she was going to push past me and sort Motto out. Instead, she spoke to me.

'What are you doing here?'

I didn't get what she meant. 'I came with M-Motto, didn't I?'

'Motto, Motto.' She almost spat the words. 'Is he the

only friend you've got?'

'Maybe.'

'Then you're even thicker than I thought. Do yourself a favour, Pete. Go find somebody else.'

'Why? Why sh-should I?'

Lorna shook her head. 'You can't see it, can you? You just can't see it. Why do you think he always comes back to you? The same reason a good-looking girl hangs around with a plain one. To make her shine. He likes you around because you make him look good.'

She stalked away from me then, slamming her own bedroom door shut.

Did I take any notice of what she'd said? Course not. I reckoned she'd just been taking it out on me because she was upset. I went into Motto's room.

'About time too,' he said. 'Come on, what d'you reckon? Think I'll get away with having my tie like this?'

He'd turned his school tie around so that the thick part was tucked into his shirt and only a thin stub was showing. 'I mean, nobody in the whole school wears their tie like this, do they...'

Chapter Four

Playing tricks with school uniform was Motto all over. If something was meant to be so, then he'd try changing it round just to be different.

The tie business was typical. Within days, every boy in the year was wearing their tie the same way. When the practice was officially denounced Motto just came up with something else – anything to look different to the rest of us.

He'd leave his shirt collar undone. He'd walk around with his tie over his shoulder. He went through a stage of pulling the cuffs of his blazer down over his hands, as if he was the Part-Invisible Man. At various times his trouser legs had vertical creases, no creases and – once – horizontal creases. When yelled at for it by Mr Stowell, our Year Tutor, he had an answer ready.

'Sailors have their trousers this way, sir. If it's good enough for the Royal Navy, it's good enough for me.'

Stowell took it in good part. 'Well, let's just put it this way, Mark. Turn up with them looking like that tomorrow – and you'll be sunk.'

Out of school he was the same. Where once he'd been pretty regular, soon it began to look as if he'd been raiding the dustbins behind the Oxfam shop. His usual outfit was a scarlet top with a hole in the elbow, and a pair of grubby jeans. And of course, where everybody else wore top-brand trainers he had a pair of khaki baseball boots with rainbow laces.

'I don't run with the herd, Pete,' he'd say.

I thought that was great. To be confident enough not to care what the world thinks, but just go out and be yourself.

It was only later – only days before what happened to him – that I finally realised what Motto really had. And it wasn't confidence at all…

'Yes, all right.' Shiner interrupts me sharply. Then, realising what he's done, he sucks in a breath before continuing. 'Do you want to tell me about how you got involved with the graf?'

The graf. With that one word his mask has slipped. It's short for graffiti, and he's an expert in it.

'Well?' he says as I hesitate.

I look at him. His soft, social worker's voice is in place again, but now he's back to the Shiner I know – the bloke I've mentally thought of as 'Shiner' ever since I saw him for the first time, sitting on a sofa polishing the badge on his policeman's helmet like Aladdin rubbing his lamp.

Just a police constable he was then, not a detective inspector like he is now.

Not that that's made a lot of difference. The way he asks

a question still makes my stomach churn. And I'm not the only one. Motto felt exactly the same way, I know.

But, like it or not, I've got to face him down. We're stuck in here together, on opposite sides of a table, and I've got to tell him the truth. The whole truth, and nothing but the truth as they say. I've got to convince him I'm innocent.

So, I force myself to look right into his eyes – into the eyes of Detective Inspector Bryan Tomlinson of London's Metropolitan Police.

'It was a j-joke,' I stutter. 'It st-started as one of M-Motto's jokes…'

Jokes had become an increasingly big part of Motto's attention-grabbing armoury. He'd turn up with the weirdest array of things, all bought from the party shop in town. Rubber spiders that he'd dangle in front of people's noses during lessons, animal masks that he'd slip on before jumping out on some unsuspecting First Year, fake sausages of dog's muck that he'd place beneath Stowell's chair.

He played that one before a History lesson – the subject Stowell took us for – and it got him dragged out to the front for an ear-bashing.

Stowell tried sarcasm. 'Do you want to be the school clown?' he asked Motto.

It was the worst thing he could have said. The laugh that went round the room made Motto's face light up.

'I didn't know the school had one, sir!' he replied

smartly, 'but if the job's going, I'll take it!'

That little episode got him a couple of after-school detentions, and a fortnight sitting under Stowell's nose for tutorials and History lessons. Maybe that's why he was listening more than usual when Stowell turned to Local History and gave us the story of Neptune.

'Neptune'. That's what everybody called the statue in the middle of Longbridge Park lake, even though it was actually an angel.

'The whole of the park was once part of the Albright family estate,' Stowell had told us, 'until, that is, the fourth Earl lost most of his fortune gambling. Realising he would have to sell the bulk of the estate to pay his debts was too much for him. He committed suicide.'

'How?' asked Motto, agog.

'He rowed out to the deepest part of the lake and jumped overboard. The statue in the middle of the lake was erected by the Earl's son as a memorial to him.'

I saw Motto's hand go up again.

'Did the Albrights have a family crest, sir?'

Stowell looked surprised, but pleased, at Motto's interest. 'Crossed keys,' he said. 'In red, on a silvery-blue background. Red and blue were the colours of the Albright livery. That means, for instance, that the servants' uniforms were in those colours.'

'Red and blue?'

'Yes.' He glared around the room. 'And the first person to mention Superman will find himself in detention faster

32

than that particular superhero could go round the globe!'

Motto grabbed me straight after the lesson. He looked as though he'd won a fortune.

'Pete, my boy, Stowell's just given me a great idea. And I mean great.'

When he told me what it was, I backed off. 'Motto. I'm not so sure…'

'Come on. It'll be a laugh. Think of the effect. The eyes that'll be popping round here when they see it.'

I suppose I was flattered at him coming my way again. He'd been going around with some of the other kids in the class of late, but after a few Motto-caused detentions they were presumably keeping him at arm's length.

'Well…'

'Pete, if you don't come in with me then it's off. Non-starter. You're the only one I know who I'd trust to be my partner.'

Motto's partner. Me and him. It was the killer blow, as he knew it would be.

'OK,' I said. 'It'll be a laugh, won't it, Motto?'

He'd put his arm round my shoulders. 'That's right, Pete. A real laugh.'

It was just before ten. Being mid-September, the sun had been down for a while although the red on the horizon was still giving off enough light to help us to see what we were doing.

We met at the eastern end of the park, near the locked

33

single gate. Motto had already climbed over the fence and was leaning against the rusty spiked railings waiting for me.

'You got your stuff?' he hissed as I clambered over to join him.

'Yes.' I patted the holdall I'd brought with me. 'Two tins of paint. One red, one blue. I knew I'd seen some in the garage.'

Motto stuck a thumb in the air. 'Well done, partner.'

He did it again as I added, 'And I found a couple of new brushes. I've never really turned it out before. I didn't know just how much stuff Dad had...'

But by the time I'd got to the last part Motto wasn't listening. He was already heading across the grass towards the southern tip of the lake.

There, beside the whitewashed boathouse, a little fenced-off section led in by a wicket gate to a wooden jetty. In the winter the flat-bottomed rowing boats you can hire are stored in the boathouse. In the summer, though, they don't bother to put them away, just leave them tied in a crocodile alongside the jetty.

We crept towards them, the boards of the jetty squeaking softly beneath our feet. I saw a problem at once – or so I thought.

'They're chained up,' I whispered.

From a solid iron post the chain was looped through the near-side rowlock of the first boat, then on to each of the other boats before ending up, padlocked again, to a second post at the other end of the jetty.

'A little chain?' said Motto, not even trying to keep his voice low. 'What's that to a determined duo like us?'

He'd got it all worked out. Bending down next to the boat at the head of the crocodile, he pulled out the screwdriver he'd brought with him.

'What are you going to do?'

'Elementary, my dear Ellis. Would you believe – undo a screw?'

Yes, that's all it needed. Undoing one of the screws holding the near-side rowlock in place, Motto simply twisted it round and the chain slipped free.

'There you go,' he said. 'Jump in, Mister Mate. Time we were paddling.'

I looked for the oars. It hadn't occurred to me that they didn't leave them in the boats overnight. When I didn't see any I said dumbly, 'How?'

'Use our hands, of course. You paddle on your side, I'll paddle on mine.'

Motto was in his element, acting out the dream he'd been having that afternoon. It wouldn't surprise me if he'd even prepared the classic Motto-ism he came out with.

'Hey, Pete!' he laughed. 'We can pretend we're facing the challenge of a single-handed race!'

He emphasised the 'single-handed' of course. Now, though, the word that sticks in my mind is 'challenge'...

Looking back now, that *was* how it felt that night – like a crazy challenge. Crazy, but serious, like the ones he'd invented in the Androids game. Except that this time I had no competition for his right-hand man.

Including course corrections and a couple of full circles it was a good twenty minutes before we reached the centre of the lake. I'd been growing more and more nervous all the way. If we were spotted, there'd be no escape. But that thought hadn't seemed to have occurred to Motto – or, if it had, he wasn't worried about it.

He was humming to himself as he dug into the folds of his jacket, pulled out a length of rope, and tied the boat to the railings surrounding the large square pedestal Neptune stood on. Then, with me following, he hopped out and on to the pedestal. Try that trick in daylight and there'd be trouble. A shrieking whistle would be followed by a signal to 'come in number whatever', even though you might only have been out for a couple of minutes. Half expecting to hear a whistle, I glanced over at the boathouse. I could barely see it through the gloom.

'Nuts,' cursed Motto. 'We could do with a torch.'

'I got one,' I said proudly, digging in my holdall and lifting it out along with the paint tins and the brushes. 'I found it in the garage as well.'

'Pete. You're a genius, kid! Where would I be without you? Come on, you hold it and I'll do the painting.'

He rubbed his hands together like a concert pianist preparing to give a performance, the whole thing a fun game. After the praise for bringing a torch I was feeling better but, even so, I still nervously shielded the beam as I held it for him to start work.

The blue went on first, slapped on hastily with short, sharp strokes. He did the angel's front, then its back and wings.

'Don't feel blue, little angel,' he laughed. 'Here comes the red.'

A few more minutes, with Motto leaning this way and that as he pretended to be an artist, and it was finished.

'Like it!' I said.

Motto had done a good job. At that moment I thought it was the funniest thing I'd ever seen.

Neptune's body was no longer coloured mould green and bird-dropping white. Courtesy of Motto, the angel was now dressed in a stunning blue all-in-one, topped off by a pair of bright red underpants.

'There you go, my angel,' grinned Motto. 'You're back in the livery of the Albright family.'

'But looking like Superman!' I hissed.

'Sheer coincidence, Pete. As you'll see when I add the Albright crest to his bum.'

On the back of the angel's red underpants Motto had carefully left unpainted an area in the shape of a pair of crossed keys. As I held the torch, he now carefully filled the space in, as if the statue was a stone colouring-in book.

'All done,' he said when he'd finished. 'Back into the boat, Number One. It's time to head for port.'

Stuffing the gear away, I stepped carefully from the pedestal and into the boat. Holding the torch, and still standing, I lit the way for him to do the same.

By now though, my nerves had almost got the better of

37

me. All I wanted was to be away from there, away from the shadows and the loud, echoing sounds Motto was making.

'Come on, man! Let's go!'

But Motto seemed to be more concerned with taking a last look at his handiwork. That's what caused the accident. Carelessly lifting a leg over the low railing he caught his foot and half stepped, half fell into the body of the boat. In an instant it was rocking wildly from side to side.

With a cry, he toppled backwards. I thought he was going to plunge straight over the stern and into the lake. But at the last moment he threw out a hand to grip the side, making the boat dip violently his way.

I lost my balance then. Desperately I tried to stop myself falling, but that only made the boat lurch even more. This time there was no way I could stay upright. Falling backwards, I let go of the torch. It splashed into the lake.

And then, before I knew it, I was following it, performing a kind of backward roll so that my legs looped over the side and into the chill water.

'Motto!' I gasped, hanging on like grim death.

I was scared, really scared. I can swim, but not well enough to cope with a load of soggy clothes. Even as I was I could feel my wet jeans starting to suck me down.

'Help me!'

He didn't move. I thought at the time he was trying to keep the boat balanced but, knowing what I know now, I reckon he was probably just too scared to move. Whatever the reason, it turned out to be the best thing he could have done. If he had tried to grab me the boat would definitely have gone over and then we'd both have been in trouble.

As it was, with Motto staying put and keeping things steady, I was able to lever myself forward with my elbows and grab hold of one of the planks that passed for seats. Heaving my soaking legs out of the water I looped myself over the side.

A quick pause to adjust my grip and take a deep breath, a second heave, and I was back into the boat again.

'You OK?' gasped Motto, sounding relieved.

I began to wring out the legs of my jeans. 'Yeah, just about.'

We thrashed our way across to the other side of the lake. Leaving the boat where it was, we legged it out of the park, separating at the bottom of Motto's road. A couple of minutes later I was indoors.

I was cold.

I was wet.

But, for some reason, I felt great.

'A mindless prank,' said Shiner. He's leaning across the table towards me, his eyes hard though he's trying to keep his voice under control. 'You're telling me it all started with that? A mindless prank.'

'Yes. But...'

'But. But what?'

He's trying to bully me and I'm not going to let him. I'm

going to tell it the way it was. I've had time to think it out, to work it out.

I'm sorry about Motto, really sorry. Maybe if I'd known what I know now, things would have been different – though I don't reckon so. It was going to happen one way or the other.

So I look across at him, shake my head. 'It wasn't m-mindless. Mindless means d-doing something without knowing why.'

'And you're telling me you had a reason?'

'Yes.'

There'd been a reason all right. Motto had known what it was all along. I only fully realised what it was the next day.

Chapter Five

Of course, we took a detour on the way to school next morning in order to view our handiwork. Motto suggested it the moment we met, and I agreed straight off. To my surprise, I wanted to see it almost as much as he did.

As we caught sight of Neptune, Motto clapped me on the back in delight.

'Look at that, kid! Just look at it!'

In the early-morning sun, what we'd done to Neptune couldn't be missed. The paint-covered statue glistened, the crossed keys crest on its backside clearly visible.

But, elated as he was, Motto's real reason for doing the job hadn't been the challenge. That's what sank in when we got to school.

I went off to hand in some homework. By the time I got back, he'd set up camp near the vending machine and was in full flow, a large crowd around him. That's what he'd really wanted out of bombing Neptune: the chance to talk about it.

'Got one of the rowing boats, didn't we? Paddled out in the dark, hit Neptune, then paddled back again. I nearly fell in and drowned a couple of times!'

41

A murmur went round the crowd. Not everybody believed what they were hearing.

'See for yourself. Neptune's now a dead ringer for Superman. We gave him a full make-over. Blue tights and the nattiest pair of red knickers you've ever seen in your life!'

The laughter spurred him on. 'And,' he said with a flourish, 'to top it off, we've even given it the Albright family crest.' He grinned as a Motto-ism flicked into mind. 'Or maybe I should say "to bottom it off", 'cos that's where we painted it – on his jacksie!'

He was winning them over. Kids were making plans to head out to have a look at it after school. And, standing there on the fringe, I liked what I heard. I won't deny it. They were talking about something I'd been part of.

Just then a group from the year above us came along the corridor. They must have heard what Motto had been saying; he hadn't been trying to keep his voice down.

Among them was Lorna. Since that day at her place she'd changed. Apart from when she was talking to her few chosen friends I'd hardly ever seen a smile on her face. Instead she wore an expression of calculated toughness.

Passing by, she didn't even look Motto's way. Jody Vahl, the girl walking beside her, couldn't resist it though. She waved a hand at Motto's audience.

'What's this, Motto? Story time for the Under Fives?'

I saw Lorna flick an amused eye at the boys behind her as Jody went on, piling on the sarcasm. 'What's today's fairy

42

tale? Don't tell me. "How I painted my masterpiece on the lake." What did you use, Motto? *Water* colours?'

The group laughed. So did some of Motto's audience. I could see that if he didn't recover the situation quickly, he'd lose them.

That's when he looked up and saw me. He grabbed at me as if I was a lifeline. 'You don't believe me? Ask Pete. He was there. Come on, Pete, you tell them. We did it together, didn't we? You and me.'

As he said it, everybody swung round to look at me. For a moment I was stunned.

I wasn't sure what to say, or how to say it – until I saw the mix of disbelief and amusement on their faces. I could almost hear them thinking. P-P-Pete Ellis? Pulling a cool stunt like this?

It was, well...a great feeling. It gave me a surge of confidence I'd never known before.

'It's the truth,' I said. 'Just like Motto said. G-go and see for yourself. We d-did it all right. The painting, the crest, the lot.'

'Tagged it as well, did you?'

Almost as soon as it had arrived, my moment had passed. Now the eyes swung towards one of the boys in Lorna's group, a self-styled toughie called Terry Quarm. Beside him, looking as if the whole business was beneath him, was his far brighter pal Karl Anstice.

As Motto hesitated, Quarm repeated the question. 'I said, did you tag it? Prove it was you, like?'

43

Still Motto didn't answer. Beside Quarm, Anstice gave a theatrical sigh. 'You've got to tag your graf, Motto. No tag, no proof. No proof, no fame.'

Quarm shook his head. 'We don't reckon you did it, Motto.'

'I did, I tell you!'

'Sorry, Motto.' Anstice had whipped out a handkerchief and was dabbing at his eyes. 'Like I say, no tag, no proof. I'd really like to believe you, but...' He pretended to blow his nose. 'I just can't! None of us can. Right, guys?'

Following his lead the whole group broke into a flurry of false wailing which turned into hoots of laughter as they all moved on down the corridor.

From over his shoulder, Quarm called, 'You want to see some real graf, Motto? Go visit the Magic Roundabout!'

I looked at Motto. Like me, I don't think he'd had a clue what Quarm had been talking about. That's why he'd not been able to stop his – our – big moment being soured.

But from the look in his eyes I knew he was going to find out.

I didn't see him again all that day. I get to have a few lessons on my own, and that happened to be a day when most of them took place.

Lessons on my own. It was something I'd hated at first. Being on my own made me feel like one of those runners you see in the Olympics distance races – you know, the ones who trail in half an hour behind everybody else. Saying they were lessons for my 'special educational needs' didn't help either. It made me feel like I was suffering from some contagious disease and had to be kept apart from everybody else while I was getting treatment for it.

Now, though, I quite enjoy them. The teachers I get are generally all right, and one-to-one it's more like having a chat than anything else. In class, it often feels like I'm playing a demon fruit machine. The teacher pulls the handle and – like the fruits – the facts go round so fast I can't tell one from the other. Even when I do get them to stop it's only to discover they've ended up in the wrong places. Orange, lemon, grape. Wrong, wrong, wrong. Another losing line.

Anyway, by the time I got out at the end of the last period, Motto had gone. I went through the park, expecting to see him taking another look at Neptune, but he wasn't there either. He'd have enjoyed it if he had been.

Word had got around. Gaggles of kids were gathered round the lake, looking out at Neptune as though it was a tourist attraction and they were sightseers. All they were missing were cameras round their necks.

A few of them nudged each other and pointed my way. Motto would have stopped and lapped it up, but I kept going.

He turned up later that evening. Mum was down for a late-night cleaning session, so she'd been home when I got there. Not having to get my own tea ready had meant I'd eaten early.

When Motto arrived I was out in the garage. He pulled

45

back the door and saw what I was doing.

'Pulling the old layout to bits, eh? Good thinking. It's probably worth a few quid from a dealer. Those engines must have set your old man back...'

I had to put him right. 'I'm not p-pulling it to bits. I'm extending it.'

He could barely stifle his amusement. 'What? You mean you still play with this stuff?'

'Why not? My dad did.'

He opened his mouth to say something, then decided not to. Instead, he came and took a closer look. 'So what you doing then?'

I wanted to tell him I was doing what I'd been doing for ages. It was just that he hadn't seen it. After his early burst of enthusiasm, Motto hadn't been fussed about using the layout.

If anything, though, I'd got even keener. The more I looked at it, the more I found to admire in Dad's craftsmanship. Like me he'd been no boffin, but that hadn't mattered. He'd produced something for which brains alone wouldn't have been enough. He'd built that layout from his heart, and I'd recently started to wonder if I couldn't do the same.

So, at those times when Motto's circle expanded and he had other kids to call on, I'd returned to my old friend in the garage.

'Longbridge Station has been extended since Dad made this,' I explained. 'So I'm t-trying to bring it up to date.'

46

As I said it, I automatically glanced over to the notice board. The newspaper photograph was now yellowing with age, but it had never crossed my mind to take it down. I wanted him to see what I was doing.

Motto puffed out his cheeks. 'Rather you than me, sunshine. They've just about rebuilt the place lately, haven't they?'

He was right. Since Dad had made the layout, Longbridge Station had been dramatically extended to create a lower level platform for District Line through trains. Now they actually dived into an underpass as they approached the station, stopped, then came spitting up on the other side of the station as they continued on their way to Upminster.

That's what I was trying to model. I'd had the idea of using moulded perspex so that the trains heading for the lower level didn't simply disappear but stayed in view.

I was explaining all this to Motto when the garage door slid open again and Mum came in.

'Come on, you two, out of the way. Some of us haven't got time to stand around nattering.'

Nudging her way between us, she headed for the shelves which lined the end wall. Dad's garage, as I'd discovered when I was looking for the tins of red and blue paint, was well organised. The cupboards and shelves were neatly stacked. Also, various things he'd used regularly – saws, hammers, spanners and the like – hung from boards with their own painted outlines so that it had been immediately obvious if anything was missing.

And something was.

'Oh...' Mum had stopped, her hand poised over an empty outline. 'Now where's that torch gone?'

The torch I'd dropped in the lake. I'd put the paint tins back, but in the excitement of the night before I'd completely forgotten about the torch.

Motto dived in, quick-witted as ever. 'It must have been stolen, Mrs Ellis. By somebody light-fingered!'

Mum hit him playfully on the side of the arm. 'Get away with you!' She turned to me. 'Peter, the bulb's gone in the cupboard under the stairs. I can't see what I'm doing and I'm late. Have you seen the torch?'

My tongue wouldn't work. All I could do was look uselessly at the outline on the board. 'I c-can't remember,' I managed finally.

'Hang on.' It was Motto, totally convincing. 'I remember now. I borrowed it, Mrs Ellis. A couple of weeks ago it was. Mum and Dad were out y'know, like usual, and I couldn't find ours. So I nipped over here. I did ask you, Pete. You had your head in the layout, remember?'

He didn't give me a chance to answer, just ploughed on, shaking his head. 'Miles away he was, Mrs Ellis. He probably didn't even realise what I'd done. I just grabbed it and shot out again. Sorry. I'll go and get it.' Motto turned for the door, then stopped with a frown. 'Assuming I can remember where I put it...'

But Mum was already pushing her way out of the garage.

48

'It doesn't matter, Mark. I haven't got time. Leave it. I'll manage.'

'Oops,' grinned Motto when she'd gone. 'You nearly dropped us in it there, Pete.' He laughed. 'Bit like your torch!'

'I'll have to g-get another one.'

'Forget it. We've got a couple. I'll bring one over and say I couldn't find the one I borrowed.'

'Won't your dad miss it?'

'He doesn't miss me and Lorna when we're not there, so I don't reckon he's going to miss a torch.'

Motto's smile faded. His eyes flickered for an instant. 'On second thoughts, maybe he would miss a torch.'

It was another of those little remarks that I now realise I took the wrong way. This one I assumed to be a joke. I knew why Motto's dad wasn't around much – everybody did, it wasn't a secret. We all assumed that Motto didn't mind. I know differently now. We all do.

'I'll go and get another torch after school tomorrow,' added Motto. The mention seemed to remind him why he'd come over in the first place. 'Hey, Pete. Come along with me. I've got something to show you.'

'What?'

'The Magic Roundabout. The place Quarm talked about, remember? I went there after school. Pete, it's something else.'

49

Chapter Six

The Magic Roundabout is what we called it, but officially it was known as the Bandstand: a raised circular dais planted slap-bang in the middle of the Memorial Gardens, its gleaming white canopy roof supported by four tall round pillars.

The Memorial Gardens were a peaceful and popular square. Their original purpose was obvious the moment you stepped through the gate. There, forming a kind of wall, carved slabs of grey granite carried the names of those who'd died in the world wars. In front of them towered a tall granite cross. There wasn't a day in the year when that cross didn't have a poppy wreath lying at its base.

But the gardens had not only been designed for remembering the dead. They had been put there for the living as well. Curving pathways skirted flower- and rosebeds, and bench seats lined the perimeter.

That's where the Magic Roundabout came in. During the summer months they'd often hold lunch-time concerts in the Memorial Gardens. Dad had enjoyed them. He'd taken me a number of times, getting a spot as close to the bandstand as he could. The music hadn't done much for me, but I'd loved the scarlet uniforms and the brass instruments gleaming in the sun.

'You got to get close,' said Motto as we arrived at the gates. 'You can't see it till you get up close. That's what's so cool about it.'

He dived off, but I stopped. Habit, I suppose. Dad had always stopped and stood for a moment, his eyes focused on the carved stone wall and the lofty cross.

They'd been hit.

Whorls of paint, random and ugly, covered the slabs, obliterating some of the names. A long slash of red wound its way round the upright of the cross. A workman was trying to clean off what he could. In front of it all stood an old woman, a wreath in her hands, her eyes wet.

Motto was almost at the Magic Roundabout. Turning to find out where I'd got to, he beckoned me over excitedly. By the time I got there he'd skipped up the double steps which ran all the way round the bandstand, and was pointing above his head.

'There. That's what Quarm was on about.'

I followed his gaze. At the peak of the Magic Roundabout's canopy, where the roof funnelled into a point, were the letters S-U-N.

'Sun? What's that mean?'

Motto explained at once. 'I've been asking around. It's a crew tag.'

I looked blank.

'A tag is a name. When you hit something – y'know, like

52

we did Neptune – you should put your tag on it. That proves you did it and nobody else. A crew tag is like it. Except it's the name of a crew. A gang,' he added, in case I still hadn't understood.

I understood all right. It was what the Android game had amounted to.

Motto looked again at the lettering. 'The other thing I found out about tags is that they're supposed to mean something.'

'Yeah? So what does SUN mean?'

'One kid in Lorna's year reckons it's short for Smart and Uncatchable.' Gazing upwards he added, 'I reckon the first bit's right, anyway. Getting up there couldn't have been easy.'

I could see what he meant. The pinnacle of the roof had to be at least three and a half metres from the ground. Reaching it would have meant climbing up to the crossbeams which supported the roof, then hanging on with one hand while wielding a spray can with the other.

Not impossible – but, with a shuddering drop to a solid floor just waiting to crack the skull of anyone who slipped, no doddle either.

'So what's the rest of it mean?' I asked Motto, for the S-U-N tag wasn't the only lettering on the ceiling.

'Obvious. They're the SUN crew's solo tags.'

One by one he pointed them out, like a stargazer identifying constellations in the night sky. There were another four tags that I could see:

CEO, sprayed in slanting capitals, the central horizontal of the E given an arrow-head which pierced the left side of the O.

ZIP, written to read vertically, from top to bottom.

HI2U, with the U turned into a grinning face.

Tel, the letters joined up, with the base of the T extending down and doing a right turn to underline the whole thing.

'A four-man gang,' I said. 'Organised.'

'Five man,' said Motto. 'There's another one. Look.'

He was right, but I was none the wiser even after he'd pointed it out. It looked like nothing more than a figure eight, but with the top of its head sliced off like so – α. It took Motto a couple of head turns before he worked it out.

'That's an alpha, I reckon. First letter of the Greek alphabet. It's often used in maths formulae.'

I took his word for it. Motto was top set for Maths whereas for me it was simply the subject in which the barrels of the fruit machine went round fastest of all.

'Alpha,' said Motto softly. 'CEO, ZIP, HI2U, Tel and Alpha. The SUN crew.'

He made it sound like he was saying a prayer.

'That did it, you know,' says Shiner. I can see he's having trouble holding his temper down about it even now.

'When the Memorial Gardens were hit, people round here finally woke up and decided to do something about graffiti

54

vandalism. From that day on, it was going to be stopped.'

He's got a big green folder on his lap, bulging with cuttings and reports. He opens it to find one particular cutting right near the front, then spins it round my way.

'See that, did you?'

I'd seen it. Motto had pointed it out at the time. It was an article from the local paper saying that to cope with the growing problem of graffiti vandalism a special Anti-Graffiti Unit was being set up. Different groups had agreed to be involved – public services, transport, the police.

At the side there was a small photograph of the officer who'd been put in charge. He's aged a bit since it was taken, or maybe he's just showing the strain of what's happened. All the same, it's clearly a picture of the man sitting opposite me. That's confirmed by the photograph's caption, which reads: 'Detective Inspector Bryan Tomlinson, who will spearhead the new Anti-Graffiti Unit.'

'You kn-knew about the SUN crew, d-did you?'

Shiner nods. 'I hadn't got any leads about who they might be, but I knew they'd been around.' He riffles angrily through the pages of the folder. 'They hadn't only hit the War Memorial, had they?'

Motto showed me that.

After visiting the Magic Roundabout we went on a tour of the town and the surrounding area. It was an eye-opener.

The SUN crew's tags were all over the show – and not just sprayed across bare walls on the corners of waste ground either, although they'd done plenty of those.

'Look. Up there!' breathed Motto as we went past the multi-storey car park.

Somehow they'd managed to hit the outside wall of the top deck. The crew tag, and all five of their individual tags, were up there for the world to see. I couldn't work out how they'd done it, but Motto had the answer.

'They must have helped each other,' he said. 'Took it in turns to stand on the wall of the floor beneath, then, while the others held him safe, leaned out to tag the wall above. Cool, or what?'

That was his reaction every time.

'That would have needed quick work,' he said when we saw the SUN crew's hit on the arch leading down into the echoing but brightly lit walkway beneath the inner ring road. 'Quick work and good organisation. There's no cover worth talking about. One of them must have acted as lookout, I reckon. Must have.'

Even a hit on the most dismal target impressed him, like the dingy grey electricity sub-station at the corner of Sheringham Avenue, just visible from the school gates. He pointed up at the triple row of barbed wire at the top of its surrounding fence, and tapped on the red warning sign with its lightning symbol.

'Dicing with death in there,' murmured Motto. 'They've got bottle, Pete. They've got guts. I've got to say that for them.'

*

56

'Guts?' says Shiner. He runs a weary hand across his eyes. 'Is that what he liked about them?'

'P-partly,' I say. 'There was m-more to it than that.'

Much more. But I'm not ready for that yet, and I don't reckon Shiner is. I'll get to that part of the story soon enough, anyway. Then we're both going to have to relive the nightmare visions of what happened to Motto.

Maybe Shiner, too, senses it isn't time, because he spins his folder round for me to see again. This time he's showing me a report form.

'Every hit the SUN crew made was recorded on a form like this,' he says. 'Information of all sorts started coming in. Incidents, security measures, you name it.'

He flips a page. 'This was the first report about you two.'

I don't need to look at it. I know what it refers to.

'The b-bus depot?'

He sighs. 'Right. The bus depot.'

Chapter Seven

After seeing the SUN stuff around town, I'd sensed a change in Motto. He talked about us doing the same sort of thing.

'Something good, though,' he said. 'Something special. It would have to be something special. Like Neptune, but...'

I knew what was coming next. The scene in school with Quarm, Anstice and Co., when his big moment had been soured, still hurt.

'...but done properly this time,' said Motto. 'With tags. We'd have to have our own tags, Pete.' And he started spending odd minutes in class doodling designs on scraps of paper that he'd quickly stuff into his pocket when the lesson ended.

Did I think the same? I suppose I did. At least, I did because I saw it was important to Motto. Just how important I discovered when we drifted into the shopping arcade one Saturday afternoon.

Normally we'd just mooch – like half the teenagers in Longbridge, or so it seemed. The arcade was the place to be seen. Gaggles of kids would spend the afternoon standing around or lolling on seats, dressed in their coolest gear and laughing a bit too loudly.

Quarm, Anstice and some of the others in Lorna's year were doing just that when we ran into them.

We'd just come out of a car accessories shop. Motto had headed for it as soon as we'd arrived. I'd followed, not thinking too much about why he should want to go in there. Then I saw him go over to the spray cans of touch-up paint – the stuff motorists use to cover up little chips and scratches in their car's paintwork – and it slowly sank in.

The checkout assistant was a lot sharper. 'I hope these aren't going to be used for anything silly,' she said as Motto handed over his money.

Motto gave her a blank look. 'How do you mean?'

'You know what I mean. Graffiti.'

A grin, and a quip. 'Not unless my dad's into it. He wants them for painting his model railway layout.'

I flinched at his words, but said nothing. He hadn't meant to hurt me. He'd just said the first thing that came into his head.

Then, as I say, we ran into Lorna's lot. She wasn't with them, but I spotted Jody Vahl perched on a seat next to Karl Anstice. Lounging near them were Terry Quarm and a few others I recognised.

It was Quarm who made the first move. As Motto went past, not noticing that he was there, Quarm reached out and snatched the bag from his hands.

'Cans, Motto?' he sneered, delving inside. 'What you planning to do with these, then? More anonymous graf?'

Hearing him, Anstice left Jody Vahl and came over. Amused, he plucked out the till receipt the shop assistant had stuffed in with the cans.

'And you *bought* them? Mot-to. Don't you know anything? Taggers don't buy their cans. They nick 'em. Ain't that so, Lorn?'

From somewhere in the arcade, Lorna had arrived to join the laughing group. She didn't join in with the fun, though. Angrily thrusting the holdall she was carrying across to Jody Vahl, she snatched the can from Quarm's fingers and tried to drag Motto away.

'Go on, Lorna,' Jody called out, laughing, her red-lipped mouth open wide. 'You tell him! Tell him Mummy and Daddy wouldn't like it!'

Lorna silenced her with a glare, then turned to Motto. But her brother was in no mood to be shoved around. Twisting away, he spun round on Quarm and the rest.

'You wait. You'll see. We'll show you!' He turned to me then. 'Won't we, Pete?'

Caught up in the fire of it all, the only thing to register with me was that he was outnumbered and needed support. 'Y-yeah!'

'Motto and P-P-Pete,' hooted Quarm. 'The dynamic duo!'

This time Lorna gripped Motto's arm, her eyes blazing. She looked more than ready to drag him away if necessary, but she didn't have to. Deciding he'd had enough, Motto allowed her to move him out of earshot of the others.

'Mark,' she hissed. 'Leave it alone.'

Motto shrugged her off. It was if he hadn't heard her. 'I *will* show them. I will.'

Lorna gripped his arm again, but this time it looked to me as though it was more in fear than anger.

'I said leave it! You don't know them like I do.'

Again Motto shrugged her off, this time to look her in the eyes. 'Get out of my life, Lorna. Right out!'

She glanced up at him and, for a moment, didn't move. Then it was as if she'd frozen over. Without a word she turned on her heel and stalked back to her grinning friends.

I followed Motto out, saying nothing as he muttered over and over again, 'I'll show them. I'll show them...'

It took him a few days to come up with an idea but, after the episode in the arcade I hadn't doubted that he would. What did give me a jolt, though, was the idea itself.

He sprang it on me during our Art lesson. Art and Design, they're my good subjects. It must be the sort of brain I've been landed with. I can't calculate to save my life, but I can draw and construct things – like the layout at home – no problem. I can see a picture in my head and bring it to life.

Anyway, I'm in with everybody else for Art and it was halfway through one of the lessons that Motto had the idea. Our teacher, Ms Halley, had just finished her regular half-hour of chat and we'd split into pairs, Motto and me, to get on with a practical. Ours was to explore light and shade. I'd found us a good spot by the window, where a narrow shaft of sunlight was slanting in and giving a really nice effect.

Motto hadn't seemed too keen. For some reason, he always preferred to find a spot in the centre of the room. But there wasn't any sunlight streaming into the centre of the room, so he'd had to come over with me. Even so, he'd seated himself slightly away from the window.

Until, that is, he saw it. Then he stood up and, after making what looked like an almost conscious effort, moved up close to the glass.

'Pete. Look. Down there.'

A glance Ms Halley's way to check that she was doing her usual and catching up on some marking, then I joined him.

I looked down. And I mean down. The building we were in, C Block, is four storeys high and the Art room is up on the third. It overlooks South Park Drive, the road which runs north–south past the school. It's a beaten-up building, always going to be repointed, repainted, re-everything, but never actually making it.

But, ugly as it is, it looks a classic compared to the bus depot over the road. It was this square, red-brick monstrosity that Motto was pointing towards.

'See it?' he whispered.

'The depot?'

'Not the depot. The bus.' Across the way, a double-decker bus was nosing its way out into the traffic. 'What do you reckon?'

'What do I reckon about what?'

'Bombing that.'

I still wasn't with him. 'The bus, you mean?'

'What do you think I mean,' he hissed, 'the white lines down the middle of the road? Yes, the bus. That bus.'

Below us, the double-decker growled its way round the roundabout and turned into South Park Drive. We watched as it squeaked to a halt beneath us, its engine thrumming.

Up at the front, Ms Halley had decided it was time she paid closer order. Putting down her marking, she set off on a lap of the room. As we turned back to our easels, I thought it through.

The bus Motto was talking about was the school service. Every day it arrived there, waiting for a good ten minutes until the bell went and kids piled out and on to it. But what was he suggesting?

'Hit the inside, you mean?' I whispered.

Motto shook his head. 'Use your imagination, kid. Not the inside. The outside! On top, even. See?'

Leaning over, I took a look down at the roof of the bus. 'The top? You're joking!'

'No, I'm not,' hissed Motto. 'Think about it. Our tags on that bus, sitting outside the school for everybody up here to see. It's perfect!'

Perfect, maybe. But there was an obvious problem.

'How do we know which one to go for? There must be a dozen buses they use on that route.'

He'd got the answer to that one. 'Not on the school run

there aren't. They don't trust our lot with a decent bus. Check out the number plate, go on. It's a K reg, I bet. They use the same one every day.'

I checked. A K reg it was. Ten years old if it was a day.

'But – how do we get at it?' I said.

'The only way possible,' he said. 'While it's in the depot. I tell you, security down there is as flabby as a beer gut.'

'You mean...break in there?' I hissed. 'Break in and bomb that bus?'

I shook my head. This wasn't like the Neptune hit. What he was suggesting was different league. 'I don't know, Motto. Breaking in...'

He grabbed at my arm, his voice excited and urgent. 'Hey, Pete. I'm with you. I don't want to know if it's a break-in job. But it might not be. At least let's check it out, eh?'

I paused as Ms Halley drew near us, then, as the end-of-school buzzer sounded, hurried away again to begin packing up. By the time she'd gone, I was gazing out of the window again, down at the bus, imagining how it would look with massive tags along its side. On the roof, even, assuming Motto had been serious.

He came up behind me. 'What do you reckon? Check it out, shall we? You and me?'

You and me. Me and you.

'OK,' I said finally.

Chapter Eight

Checking the place out was easy, ridiculously easy. As Motto pointed out, we were able to tackle it from two directions.

'Start at the front and act normal,' he said. 'Unless they're mind readers as well as bus drivers they're not going to know what we're thinking, are they?'

So that's what we did. By simply wandering up and down the road outside the depot we found out plenty.

The building itself had large IN and OUT openings, with metal shutter doors which rolled down from the top. Cavernous as it was, though, it clearly wasn't big enough. A further opening at the side of the depot building led out on to a wide expanse of concrete. To block this opening there was a huge, wheeled, concertina-like panel which could be rolled into place. Once that was across, and the front shutters down, I couldn't see a way in at all.

The expanse of concrete had to be an overflow area. During the day, we'd noticed, it was littered with more cars than buses, obviously owned by drivers and other staff. When we checked it late one night, though, the position was reversed. The cars had mostly gone, and the place was crammed with buses.

'Two big problems, then,' said Motto, like he was planning an assault on an enemy stronghold. 'One, we'd need to get over that fence.'

'Without being ripped to bits,' I added. The overflow area was fronted by a steel fence with a triple loop of razor wire on top.

'And two,' continued Motto, 'finding some cover when we're in there.' The whole of the overflow area was covered by floodlights mounted on the wall of the depot building.

Checking the depot out from the second direction – the rear – was equally easy. Longbridge is one of the few local schools that haven't sold off their playing fields. There's enough space on them for a couple of football pitches and half a dozen tennis courts. More importantly, those courts back on to the fence surrounding the bus depot.

Wandering round there at lunch time, Motto immediately saw the answer to one of the problems.

'There's an easy way in!'

A section of the fence had been curled up by tennis players who'd hit wayward shots into the depot and weren't prepared to kiss their ball goodbye. Squeezing under it would be no problem. I was about to mention the fact that the rear area was also covered by floodlights when he added thoughtfully, 'Or it could be a way out. Look over there.'

In the depot's rear wall was a small door. It had no handle on the outside and, in the time we'd spent watching, it hadn't been opened once. Another check, this time by strolling past the front of the depot building, confirmed that it had a bar across it. The door was a fire exit.

'What if it's alarmed?' I said.

'It isn't,' said Motto confidently. 'I know it isn't. Like I know you can ignore those signs.'

Two large signs mounted on the front of depot fences advertised the fact that the depot was protected by dog patrols. 'The contract ran out two weeks ago. They haven't renewed it yet. There aren't any security guards.'

'How on earth do you know that?'

He winked. 'Believe me. I just know, right?'

I didn't argue. From the way he said it I had a good idea where he'd got the information, and I was still struggling with what he was suggesting.

'So you want us to get in the b-back way and not worry about the security lights?' I said.

'No,' said Motto. 'You're forgetting. We want to hit the K reg and I haven't yet seen that end up in the overflow.'

He was right. Over a period of a week we'd seen that same bus come back to near enough the same spot in the cavern each day. Not once had we seen it moved to the outside.

'So what d-do we do? Hit another one?'

'No.' Motto's voice was hard. 'I don't want to hit another one. I want to hit that one.'

It shouldn't have been a surprise. That K reg was the only bus he could be sure would stop right outside the school.

I was missing something, though. I tried to get it clear.

'But once the d-depot's shut, there's no way in.' I looked at him, wondering if he was changing his line. 'You're not suggesting we get in through that fire door?' I began to get agitated. 'No break-ins, Motto, you s-said no break-ins...'

'Calm down, Pete. We're not going to get in that way. That's the way we get out afterwards.'

'Afterwards? So how do we g-get in?'

He laughed like crazy. 'Obvious, isn't it! We catch a bus!'

So, what was Motto's plan? Like he said, to catch a bus.

He got hold of a timetable. A quick scan of routes and times told him that a number 387 would do the job nicely. A classic red London double-decker, it ran close to where we lived, then wound out in a large arc around the town before turning back in to head for the depot.

'If we catch it a distance from the depot,' explained Motto, 'the driver will have forgotten all about us by the time he gets there.'

We set about watching the comings and goings at the garage for a few nights. Most times I was there and back before mum got home. Same with Motto and his parents.

If there was a chance of being quizzed we played one off against the other.

'I'll be going over to Motto's this evening. We're working on an Art project together.'

He said the same. 'I'll be over at Pete's house. We've got an Art project to do.'

So, with our alibis squared up, we logged the way traffic came and went at the depot. The last official bus stop was fifty metres or so short of the IN gap. After pulling up, the driver would get out of his seat and bellow up the stairs to anybody who'd nodded off or had their nose in a book and hadn't realised where they were. Sometimes drivers actually marched up the stairs to have a look for themselves before jumping into the cab again and pulling in to the depot. But not once had we seen a driver go right to the back of the top deck to check there.

Motto decided we were ready. 'We go Thursday. Right?'

I nodded. Mum was in the middle of a long spell of nights. Getting out wouldn't be a problem. 'That b-best for you, is it?'

'Any night's best for me,' he said.

'You don't mean that.'

'Don't I just,' said Motto angrily. 'Dad hardly shows his face during the week. Half the time I only run into him at weekends.'

'What about your mum?'

'Soup run, as usual,' said Motto curtly. 'Still, at least I know how to get her attention if I want it. All I've got to do is doss down in a shop doorway. She'll be roaring up with a blanket and hot drink in no time at all.'

When he made cracks like these I didn't know what to say. I couldn't understand why he felt so bad. I wanted to tell him that at least he had two parents, but I couldn't.

'How about L-Lorna?' I said, finally.

He laughed, without joy. 'Lorna goes for a regular sleep-over at Jody's on Thursdays. And any other night she can get away with it.'

*

We caught the bus at just before midnight, three miles out. After paying a fare to take us halfway round the circuit, we clomped upstairs. Being the last bus there were a lot of getting-ons and jumping-offs; certainly far too many for the driver to keep tabs on whether or not we'd got off when we should.

Upstairs, we spread ourselves across the back seats so as to make sure anybody still on the bus when it came to last stop would have to get off before us. We needn't have worried. With two stops to go we were on our own.

'Going down,' whispered Motto cheerfully.

Sliding down on to the seat so that he was half lying and half sitting, he pulled his rucksack under his head. On the other side of the aisle I did the same. From the top of the stairs at the front there was no way we could be seen. Only by the driver coming right up the aisle and looking down on top of us could we have been spotted.

But would he? There was no escape if he did. The bus set off to complete the final half-mile of its journey.

'Last stop coming up,' hissed Motto. 'Pretend you're asleep.'

He closed his eyes. I did the same as I felt the bus slow, then lurch to a halt. Almost immediately, the driver was yelling up the stairs.

'Depot!'

I held my breath, waiting for the bus to start up again. Suddenly footsteps began clumping up the stairs. Heart racing, I glanced across at Motto. Cool as you like, he was still pretending to be asleep.

72

The footsteps halted as the driver, probably just a few stairs up, decided it wasn't worth the effort. A second, half-hearted, shout of 'Depot!' and he was clumping down again. Seconds later the lights went out.

'Hold very tight, please!' hissed Motto.

The bus moved off again. I felt the lurch as it turned sharp left and swung into the depot, the rackety sound of its engine bouncing off the cavern walls. In quick succession after that came a squeak of brakes, the engine being switched off, the hiss of the doors as the driver hopped out, a shout of welcome, footsteps – and, finally, an eerie quiet.

'Keep down, there'll be more to come yet,' Motto whispered, reminding me of what he'd gleaned from his timetable studying.

For the next twenty minutes we stayed tucked where we were, hardly breathing, as other buses came in from their various routes, their engines revving as they were reversed into position, then turned off for the night.

Above us, through the rear window, I could see the dome-shaped lights dangling from the depot ceiling.

Motto checked his watch. 'Not long now,' he said.

Finally I heard the clanking of the metal shutter doors being rolled down. Footsteps echoed, then came a lower rumbling as the concertina panel between the depot building and the overflow area was wheeled shut. The dome lights flicked off. Finally, a door slammed shut, the sound fading to nothingness.

In the silence Motto gave a hiss of triumph. 'Pete! We are in, kid!'

He eased himself upright. I did too, feeling my whole body pounding with nerves and excitement. Sitting on the rear seat, I looked out – and was surprised at how much I could see. Moonlight and, I guessed, some of the brightness from the blazing security lights outside, was coming in through a number of clear panels in the roof.

'Enough light to work by,' I said. 'No need to find the switch.'

'Just as well,' grunted Motto. 'We're going to have enough trouble finding our target.'

I'd never have believed so many buses could have been fitted into the space. It seemed like they'd been squeezed in with just centimetres on either side.

Hearts pounding, we edged our way down the stairs – and a surge of panic.

'The doors! He's shut the doors! How we going to get out?'

In front of us, the bus's automatic doors were firmly shut. In all Motto's planning he hadn't considered the obvious. How to get off the bus once the driver had left it.

He didn't know the answer, I could tell from the look on his face. 'There must be a way,' he said. 'Emergency exit, something like that.'

I wasn't listening, I know that. Nerves shredded by the waiting, I just babbled. 'What if there isn't? What if the driver's got to have his k-key in the ignition? What—'

'So we force them open!' shouted Motto. 'Cool it!'

He got up close to the double doors. I moved next to him, ready to add my weight, as he looked up and down at where the doors joined, looking for the best spot to force open.

And then he laughed, pointing. 'Alternatively, we could press that button.' Above the doors, so small we hadn't noticed them before, a pair of green and red buttons were labelled 'open' and 'close'.

Even so, his hand was shaking as he reached up and punched the green one. With a fierce hiss, the doors bounded open and we leaped out. We paused, breathing heavily, as the sound echoed eerily round the cavernous depot. I glanced Motto's way. Stupid as the moment had been, he'd already stopped laughing. He was as nervous as me.

Now that we were out on to the depot's oily floor, breathing in the smell of diesel, I realised that the buses weren't packed quite as closely together as they'd looked. There was perhaps half a metre to play with on either side. If this part of Motto's planning worked out, half a metre would be enough.

'Over there!' he hissed.

Motto had spotted it. Parked slightly off line, the K reg plate was visible at the far end of the bus alleyway we were standing in. Holding our rucksacks in front of us, we squeezed our way through to it.

'All present and correct,' he said as he unloaded our collection of spray cans.

I pulled out the long length of rope that Motto's plan needed. 'You want to go up first?' I said.

'Not me, Pete,' said Motto quickly. 'You can have the roof.'

'But…' The roof had been Motto's idea. It was only right he should have it.

He waved a hand. 'Call it a reward for coming in with me. I'll do a piece on the side.'

Looking back now, I can see he was making it sound like he was doing me a favour. It was only later I found out the real reason.

Decision made, we moved quickly. Motto anchored one end of the rope to a point in the centre of the K reg. Then, like a discus thrower, he hurled the rest of it over the top towards me. A quick yank to test that it wouldn't give way then, rucksack on my back, I was heaving myself up the side of the bus like a mountaineer scaling a rock face.

It was a long way. A double-decker is higher than it looks. When I reached the top I hauled myself forward and lay flat on the roof panting in triumph.

'Pete Ellis, first kid to climb Mount K reg!' crowed Motto. 'Go on, kid. Go for it!'

I unloaded my cans and got started. Down below, I could hear, Motto was already at work, the hiss of his spray can cutting through the dead quiet of the depot cavern. As for me, I didn't need to think much. I'd planned my tag and practised it on countless scraps of paper that – on Motto's advice – I'd flushed away afterwards. It was going to be in large, shadowed lettering, all laid on a silver-burst background to make it really stand out from a distance. Like I say, Art was my good subject and I was going to make the most of it.

Down below me, I knew, Motto's piece was going to be a comet's tail of colour on the near side of the bus, the side visible from the school.

We finished at virtually the same instant. 'Motto!' I called, not realising until then how dry my mouth had become with the tension. 'I'm coming down!'

Clinging to the rope, I abseiled down the side away from Motto's artwork and down to the ground. No sooner had I landed than he was by my side. We looked at each other. Then grinning in triumph, he gave me a high five.

'Yeah!' he cried.

That was as far as it went. The echoing of his voice in the gloom brought us sharply back to what we had to do next – get out, fast. Still, so long as there was no problem with the fire door, that at least was going to be nice and easy.

Slamming our gear back into our rucksacks, we zig-zagged between the buses and across to the fire door. Motto got there first. I held my breath as he leaned hard on the bar. It gave with a sharp click.

No problem!

I edged close behind him as he gingerly pushed the door open – only to have him swing round and almost knock me over as he cried out in alarm.

'Get back!'

Chapter Nine

Even as he said it, fear in his voice, Motto snatched himself away from the door and flattened himself against the wall.

Terrified, I did the same. Through the crack between the door and the frame I'd just seen what he'd seen. The floodlit overflow area to the rear of the depot building was being bombed.

I counted four of them. Dressed identically, with dark trousers and tops, each had a ski-mask pulled down over their heads, making them look like a group of terrorists on the attack.

Motto sounded afraid and awed in equal measures. 'It must be the SUN crew,' he breathed.

There was no doubt about it. Across the yard one bus already had a massive SUN tag emblazoned across its side and another was getting the same treatment from one of the crew. At the same time the other three were swarming in and out of every bus they could, covering them with their tags. Big, scrawled, unmissable tags. I could see them all.

CEO, ZIP, HI2U, Tel.

But they weren't just tagging. A window went crashing as a brick was heaved through it. Then one of them, his dark ski-mask pulled tight over his head, dived up to the top deck of the bus he was bombing. Undoing the emergency window above the back seat, he kicked it out and sent it crashing to the ground. Then, leaning out, he sprayed a large, clear tag on the back end of the roof.

An alpha.

I glanced at Motto. Open-eyed, open-mouthed, he looked like a kid who was watching a firework display for the first time. Me, I'd seen enough.

'Motto. Let's move.'

'They'll spot us.'

'No they won't, they're too b-busy. We can be out and under that fence b-before they know it.'

Even as I said it, I knew I was sounding more hopeful than I felt. Maybe I just didn't want to think about what might happen if they caught us.

Over the way, Alpha had raced down and joined the others. The whole crew were moving away from us now, rampaging through the buses like locusts attacking a field of corn. Leaning across Motto, I eased the door open a fraction more. We had a clear run across to our escape route under the fence.

Motto paused for one final look at the carnage going on. Then, ducking low, we launched ourselves out into the glare of the floodlights and sprinted across the concrete like escaping prisoners.

We were spotted just as we reached the fence.

Why neither of us had worked it out I don't know. Even

a total maths gonk like me should have managed it. There'd always been five tags whenever the SUN crew bombed a place, but I'd only spotted four of them tagging those buses. Why? Because the fifth was on lookout duty.

Dressed in the same black crew uniform, ski-mask pulled down so far that not even a glimpse of neck was visible, this one was patrolling the fence and couldn't have been more than five metres away as we reached it.

I couldn't stop myself. 'Motto!' I cried.

He saw the lookout himself then, and gave a cry of fear. Instantly, the lookout spun round, but must have been as stunned as we were. There was no shout for help, nothing, just a pair of staring eyes.

For a moment it must have looked as if we were frozen. But inside my mind was whirling. What should we do? Jump him, hit him before he shouts? No, that would get the rest of them over faster than anything.

The lookout made the decision for us. Turning – because he was outnumbered two to one I assumed – he started running towards the others. It was our chance.

Driven by fear, I dived for the gap at the bottom of the fence. Moments later I'd scrambled through and was hauling Motto through as he followed behind me.

Then we ran. Ran and ran, into the dark night, not looking back.

I felt the wind in my face. And slowly I felt something else. The further we went, the more I felt the gnawing fear being swamped by surge after surge of elation.

When finally we stopped, panting for breath, I could tell that Motto was feeling the same way. With clenched fists he punched the air. 'We did it! We did it, kiddo!'

Me – I simply looked up at the stars and screamed at the top of my voice, 'Yes! Yes!'

I'd never felt better in my whole life.

The feeling was still there when I woke next morning. How can I describe it? The best I can do is to say it was a bit like the feeling you get with one of those hairy theme-park rides. When you're on it, when it's happening, you're scared stiff. I'd been scared in that bus depot, no question about it. But when you get off one of those rides, how do you feel? Brilliant. You've survived it. You're walking on air. That's close to how it felt after that raid.

Seeing the results of it simply doubled the buzz. Word had got about during the morning, especially from kids who'd been having lessons up in the Art room and had the best view of the results.

'The SUN crew...'

'Bombed the bus depot...'

'You want to see the mess!'

Keeping quiet, waiting for the afternoon was almost too much. I'd wanted to spread the word but Motto had talked me out of it, not wanting to take the chance.

'Just in case they've cleaned it off, Pete...'

But I could see he was aching with the tension. When the afternoon finally came and we got up into the Art room ourselves, Ms Halley found she was fighting a losing battle. Every time a bus pulled out from the depot, the whole class swung round to look at it.

And, usually, there was something to look at. The SUN crew had hit so many there'd obviously been no time for the bus people to do more than start on a clean-up operation. Those they'd had a go at were passable, but the shadows of the graffiti were still visible.

Others they'd not even got around to. One pulled out with a huge SUN crew tag emblazoned on its side, its windows tagged individually in various colours: CEO. ZIP. HI2U. Tel. Alpha.

Nudges. Pointing. Laughter. Comments, not even low enough to class as a whisper.

'Look at that!'

'Wipeout!'

As the afternoon wore on, my stomach was churning. Would it come out? What if it had been pulled from service? All that planning. All that danger. All that fear. Wasted…

The clock crawled round. And then, suddenly, it was coming out. Maybe because it was ancient, or just a school service bus, or because – unlike the others – it had been tucked away in the depot building, it hadn't been given any sort of clean-up. It was just as we'd left it.

Motto's comet was still winding its way along the length of the side. It was the design I'd seen him working on. At its head was a circle, like an O, inside which he'd put the letter M – MO, being short for Motto as he'd explained it.

Spinning out from that firebrand head, his comet's tail was a wild burst of colour.

The bus stopped. And there, up on the roof, shining out from its silver-burst background, I saw it – my tag.

Beautiful.

Knowing looks were fired our way, first from those nearest the window then, as the rest of the class crowded across to look, from everybody else.

Deciding that if she couldn't beat us she should join us, even Ms Halley came over to look for herself.

'Pathetic,' she said, shaking her head.

'The others were, miss,' somebody said to her. 'Not that one, though. That's something else.'

'Special,' said another.

A murmur of agreement went round the room. More grins at Motto and me. More fame.

'It's just graffiti,' snapped Ms Halley, irritably moving everybody away from the window. 'Come on, all of you. Back to work.'

We obeyed, but our minds had gone walkabout. After another minute Ms Halley accepted that she'd lost us and declared the lesson over. The stampede back to the window started before she'd even left the room, and nobody left until our bus finally roared off.

I stayed, watching until my tag was out of sight.

My tag.

DROID.

*

'Droid?' queries Shiner.

'Like in D-droid of the Week. You know, the Android game.'

'Why?'

I shrug. 'It just seemed a good tag. We were playing a game. That's what I thought. Just playing a g-game.'

He pauses before saying what I know must be going through his head. 'It didn't stay that way much longer, did it?'

'No.'

Outside, the raid was the only topic of conversation. In next to no time, we found ourselves surrounded by kids wanting to know the details of how, when and where. Motto was in his element as he told the tale.

'Right, Pete?' he'd ask after describing every piece of the action.

Inside I'd feel a surge of delight as, for that moment, the attention swung to me while I confirmed his story – usually with not much more than a 'Right,' or a 'Sure thing.' I even found myself doing it when Motto got carried away and threw in bits about us dodging Alsatian dogs and security guards.

Delight. That's what I felt all right. If I hadn't been so wrapped up in it all, maybe I'd have seen what was coming. Seen that, in hitting the same target as the SUN crew, we'd broken an unwritten law.

The signs were there that day as Motto boasted and together we soaked up the glory.

For we weren't the greatest in the eyes of everybody. No

way. That was obvious from the reaction he got when Terry Quarm and the rest of the group from Lorna's year came past.

'See that bus, did you?' crowed Motto in their direction. 'Tags clear enough that time were they?'

Quarm did nothing more than curse as the group of boys and girls slowed but didn't stop. Only Karl Anstice spoke. And what he said sent a chill through me.

'Everybody saw the tags, Motto,' called Anstice. He stopped then, a smile on his face, before adding, 'including the SUN crew.'

'The SUN crew,' says Shiner. 'You didn't have any idea who they were?'

'None,' I say. 'Only that there were f-five of them.'

'And you knew their tags.'

'Right. CEO, ZIP, HI2U, T-Tel and Alpha. No idea what they st-stood for or anything, though.'

Shiner sighs, as if he can't believe how dumb Motto and I had been. 'And you'd never heard about turf wars – tagging on another crew's patch? You hadn't thought what that could lead to?'

'No. N-never. Not until they hit us…'

Chapter Ten

I spent most of the following weekend working on the layout.

Does that sound odd? Maybe it was. Maybe at the time I was two people: Dr Jekyll, the home kid, working on his model railway; and Mr Hyde, the tagging horror. Maybe we're all two people in our different ways – the good person and the bad one.

Whatever the explanation, my working on the layout carried on regardless. The extension, the underground platform, was taking shape. I'd finished most of the lower level and was well into making the underpass sections which would house the track.

Mum would often come in with a drink for me and sit there chatting while I got on with it. In the past I'd enjoyed it, but not recently. Maybe because, deep down, I was feeling bad about what I'd been getting up to – I don't know. All I did know was that she'd invariably swing the conversation round to Dad.

She did that Sunday afternoon. Looking back, I can't say there was any one thing she said that triggered me off. I reckon it was just an explosion that was waiting to happen.

'This is good,' she'd said, looking at what I'd done. She ran her fingers over some of the original buildings, as if she could feel the touch of the hands that had made them. 'If your dad was here he'd be really proud.'

'Would he?' I said, feeling the first pang of irritation.

'Of course he would.'

'Why? H-how do you know?'

'Why do you think? He was always bringing you out here, you know he was. He hoped you'd get the same enjoyment from it that he had.'

I rubbed harder at some sand-papering, trying to keep my cool. 'I enjoyed it b-because I was with him.'

Mum came close. I felt the touch of her hand on my arm. 'You're like him, you know.'

'No, I'm not!'

The suddenness of it shocked me. But as she said that it was like a fuse had gone off in my head. Once I'd started, I couldn't stop.

'I'm not like him!' I yelled. 'If I ever have a son, I'll care for him more than he c-cared for me!'

Mum stepped back, uncomprehending. 'What are you talking about? Your dad loved you, you know he did.'

'Then why did he get himself k-killed? If he l-loved me so much, why did he go and get himself k-killed?'

'He didn't. Peter, you know what happened...'

As she spoke the scene flashed into my mind's eye, just as it had time and time again over the years. In class, in bed, in my dreams.

88

That train, thundering towards him as he struggled with the shattered brickwork on the track. The sudden awareness he must have had, that if he didn't leave it quickly he'd be hit.

What had gone through his mind? Hadn't he thought about me?

'He could have s-saved himself!' I cried.

He could have left it. There was a good chance the train would have smashed it to one side and been none the worse for it. Even if that hadn't been the case, if the train had been derailed and people killed, nobody would have blamed him for jumping and saving himself.

But he hadn't. He'd stayed put, struggling with that brickwork until it was too late. Stayed put, not thinking of me, and been killed.

'Peter, he couldn't...'

'He could!' I cried, the tears coming from deep inside. 'He c-could have saved himself! And if he'd l-loved me he would have done!'

I sense a movement at my side. From the other side of the table, Shiner glances that way. We've been so focused on each other it's as if we'd both forgotten she was there.

'Peter,' says Mum gently.

She's here with us, listening to the story too. She could have stayed away but she didn't want to – even though I'm sure she knows that hearing it all isn't going to be easy for her either.

I can't face her as she says, 'You're wrong, you know.'

89

Am I? Even now — maybe especially now, after what happened to Motto — I can't see it her way. That's one set of fruits that the machine simply refuses to drop into place for me.

Mum didn't follow as I ran indoors and upstairs to my room. She simply let me be, let me calm down. When I came back downstairs, a while later, we both acted almost as though nothing had happened.

'Sorry,' I mumbled.

She simply shook her head, telling me without words that the subject was closed.

'OK if I g-go out tonight?' I asked. 'Me and Motto. There's a good film on at the Odeon.' It wasn't a lie, either. We really were going there.

'Not working on your school project this time, then?'

I glanced at her, wondered if she suspected anything. 'No.'

'What did you say it was?' she asked, busying herself with an ironing board.

The innocence of the question caught me cold. 'Geography,' I mumbled.

'I thought you said it was Art.'

Yes I had, I remembered too late. Admitting it could have got complicated, though. I stuck to the latest. 'No,' I insisted. 'Geography.'

Her eyebrows flicked for an instant, just as they had when I lied about the torch. And then it was back to normal and she was on to her movements for the week.

'I expect I'll be gone when you get home then,' she said. 'I'm on late turn tonight. And most of the coming month, I think.'

I went back upstairs to get ready. A clean white shirt and my new trousers, then it was off round to Motto's place.

The front door opened even before I reached it. Motto was there, and all ready to go. Behind him, in the hallway, his dad was looking sour. As he saw me, Motto swung round towards him.

'All right? Believe me now?' he shouted. Then, to me, 'Pete, where we going?'

I had a feeling I'd been caught in a crossfire. 'T-to the p-pictures,' I just managed to force out.

Behind him, Motto's dad aimed a finger. 'I didn't say I didn't believe you. All I asked is where you were going!'

'Asked?' muttered Motto under his breath. 'Interrogated, more like.' He cracked the front door shut and marched off quickly down the path.

'Problems?' I asked as I caught him up.

'Only the old man with his usual twenty questions. When he's working he doesn't want to know us. When he's home it's like he still doesn't want to know us – just wants to know *about* us. Where we've been, what we're doing, who we're seeing.'

'Maybe he's concerned?'

'Maybe he's still at work. Anyway, I just have to tell him I'm going with you and it shuts him up. Lorna gets it a lot worse.'

From the house, the shrill sound of his sister's voice carried out into the street. Motto glanced back.

'She's turning into a toughie, though. Either she clams up or she screams her head off at him. Whatever, she won't let on and it drives him up the wall.'

Another shout reached the road, followed by the thump-thump of a stereo being turned on at full volume in an upstairs bedroom.

'Wh-what about you?' I asked. 'Doesn't she t-talk to you?'

'Me and Lorna?' Motto shook his head. 'A couple of minutes a day, maybe. When we're sorting out what to get out of the freezer to eat. Apart from that, she goes her way, I go mine. Have done for ages.'

I remembered their scene in the shopping arcade. I'd thought that might have started it off, but it must have been going on for a while.

'How c-come?' I asked.

'How come the world is round, kiddo? It's just the way it is. The world's full of people who don't talk to each other. We just happen to have four of them living in the same house.'

For a moment I felt sadder for him than I did for myself. I wanted to tell him about the argument I'd had with Mum, thinking that in an odd way it would make him feel better, but I couldn't.

It didn't matter. Motto bounced back quickly, the way he always had.

'Come on, Pete,' he said. 'Let's go see this film. I need cheering up.'

*

The SUN crew hit us as we were walking home.

Bursting out from the trees as we passed the tiny north-west entrance to the park, they were on us before we knew it.

I felt a surge of fear, then total panic swept through me as I realised who the four dark-clad figures were. Ski-masks on their heads, just pairs of cold eyes and twitching lips visible, they looked terrifying.

Two of them came at us from each side. I caught a fleeting glimpse of a fifth figure, standing off watching. Then everything went black as a bag was thrust over my head. I lashed out wildly, landing a punch on somebody, only to get a smack in the face in return. Then my arms were wrenched angrily round behind my back and a hand clamped over my mouth.

From the scuffling and grunting going on beside me I could tell that Motto was getting the same treatment.

What did they want with us? What were they going to do? I had no doubt. We were in for a beating. But not there, not in the dark street. It seemed they had another place in mind.

'Right, you toys,' snarled a voice. 'Move!'

I was spun round and shoved forward, a pair of hands clutching me from each side. After a few metres the hands dragged me through ninety degrees to my left before shoving me on again.

Behind me I heard the clang of something metallic and Motto let out a cry.

93

'Shut your mouth!'

We were in the park, I was sure of it. They'd forced the small gate open somehow and Motto must have been hurt as we were pushed through.

'Where are you taking us?' I heard Motto say, his voice shaking.

They didn't answer, just dragged us on. Being unable to see a thing made it even worse. Were we heading for the lake?

I soon realised we weren't going there. We'd only been pushed along for about a minute when I was thrust sharply to my right. Suddenly it was no longer hard tarmac underfoot, but soft and spongy ground. Then I was shoved forward again, stumbling over tree roots, until the hands holding me dug fiercely into my arms and I was pulled to a halt.

'Far enough!'

My ears just had time to register Motto's frightened breathing as he was forced to a halt behind me. Then, as I heard the squeak of a wooden door opening, I suddenly realised where we'd been brought. In that part of the park there was a wooden refreshment hut. It was only open in the summer months, being closed and shuttered the rest of the year. We had to be there.

The moment I was pushed in, felt my feet touch on wooden floorboards, and heard the scuffling footsteps as the others followed, I knew I was right.

It only made the waves of fear increase. If they hammered us here, and then locked us in, it could be days before we were found.

'What are you g-going to do?' I cried.

'Sit them down,' said the voice of one of the SUN crew – the only voice we'd heard since they grabbed us.

We were shoved down on to the floor, our backs against the wall, our knees up under our chins. Again the same voice spoke, a chill voice that didn't quite sound natural somehow.

'Toys!' He spat the word out. 'Understand?'

Motto mumbled something I didn't catch. Whatever it was it gave them the idea that we didn't understand, because then other voices weighed in, snarling at us in quick succession so that I couldn't pick out who was talking.

'Beginners!'

'Bottle-suckers!'

'We work this area. Nobody else!'

'You've been operating on SUN turf!'

There was a brief respite, then the first chill voice spoke again. 'That's why you're here,' it said. 'To pay the price.'

Immediately we were dragged to our feet again, our hands twisted tight behind our backs. This was it. I waited for the first punch to land, for the pain to begin.

But it didn't happen. Instead, from my right I heard the muffled sounds of a bag being opened, followed by a light clinking noise. By then, I'd have recognised that sound anywhere. It was the clinking of spray cans knocking together as they were unloaded.

That's when I realised we weren't going to be beaten up.

They were going to teach us a lesson, all right – but in a different way.

Chill Voice spoke once more, and again I had the unmistakable feeling that it was a voice he was putting on.

'This is the price,' he said. 'Blitz them!'

It began slowly. There was a hissing beside my ear, then the feeling of paint splattering on the side of my neck and shoulder. I struggled, twisting and turning away from where the paint was coming from, and got a punch in the kidneys as a reward. There was no escape.

I felt another burst, this time sweeping down and across the front of my shirt. Then more paint landed, jetting a path down and across my legs in wild spurts.

From the hissing beside me I could tell that Motto was receiving the same treatment.

A final flourish, then it changed round. More spraying but, I sensed, from a different hand. Then another, then another, until I could feel the stickiness of it all seeping through to my skin, the whole blitz carried out in an icy silence except for the sinister hissing of the cans.

'Enough!' It was Chill Voice again, stationed somewhere to my right.

The spraying stopped immediately. What happened then I couldn't tell, but I thought I heard a shuffling, followed by an indistinguishable murmur from one of the others which might have been 'No,' but could have been anything.

Whatever it was, after a short interval I heard footsteps coming towards us from that direction, not stopping till their owner was behind us. I heard the tell-tale rattle of a spray can being shaken.

Motto got hit first. Then whichever crew member it was stepped to the side, to stand behind me. I felt a circular wave of paint land between my shoulder blades but no more, the burst of spraying over almost as soon as it had begun.

The blitz had ended.

Gripped again, we were turned round and shoved out of the hut. I heard the solid clunk of a padlock being secured before we were given our final barked warning. It came from Chill Voice without a doubt

'Tag on SUN turf again and it'll be the last time.'

With that the bags were pulled off our heads and we were both sent sprawling in the dirt. By the time we looked up they were away, dodging between the trees, their clothes and masks melting into the blackness.

Gasping, we struggled to our feet. We were in a right mess, but unhurt. Relief surged through me, making my legs buckle so that I almost fell again.

'You OK?' said Motto.

'Just about. You?'

'Yeah.' He was gasping but, if anything, sounding calmer than he had earlier. 'Let's go to your place, eh?'

Back home, I found an almost full bottle of white spirit on a shelf in the garage. Helping each other, we cleaned off the majority of the paint from our hands and necks before heading indoors for a scalding hot shower to remove some more.

'You got anything I can put on, Pete?' said Motto,

97

strangely cool as he picked his clothes off the newspaper I'd strewn on the bathroom floor. 'I can't go home in this lot.'

I found a pair of jeans he could squeeze into, though the legs ended way above his ankles. I didn't have a shirt that fitted him, so he had to settle for an old red and cream sweatshirt from the bottom of my wardrobe. Motto slipped into it. Then, clutching his ruined gear, he headed for home.

Stuffing my own paint-sodden clothes in a carrier bag, I took them outside and dumped the whole lot in the bin, piling a few newspapers on top to make sure it was well out of sight.

Before ditching them, though, I'd inspected them. They'd been given the same treatment as Motto's, meaning that – just as I'd expected – they hadn't simply been trashed by the SUN crew. They'd been tagged.

They were all there. Four of them were splattered in different places and appeared more than once. CEO, ZIP, HI2U and Tel.

Only the fifth appeared just the once. It was on my shirt, slap-bang in the middle of the back, between my shoulder blades. The last tag, the one that had ended the punishment.

Alpha.

Chapter Eleven

'And that didn't put you off?' asks Shiner.

'A b-bit, yes.'

'Only a bit?' He looks incredulous.

I wish I could say more. I wish I could say it put me off completely, put me off so much that I'd never wanted to have anything to do with tagging again.

If that had been the case then maybe everything would have been different. What happened wouldn't have happened and Motto would still...

If, if, if.

If – it's no good thinking that way. What's done is done, and I can't turn the clock back however much I'd like to.

'More than a b-bit,' I say. 'A l-lot.'

'But you still didn't stop?' says Shiner. 'You still carried on?'

I look across at him. He's struggling to make sense of it all, and I know he won't be able to unless I tell him the next part. It's the part I knew we'd get to in the end. I force the words out.

'No. Motto t-talked me round.'

'Talked you round?'

'Yeah. It didn't put him off, see. It p-pushed him further in.'

*

It was the morning after the Sun crew's attack. I was almost ready to go out of the door when Mum came downstairs.

'Don't forget I'll be late tonight,' she said, bustling from one side of the kitchen to the other.

'Right.'

'And don't forget you said you'd call in at the supermarket for me. I won't have time today. There's the list.'

I snatched up the list from the top of the fridge and stuffed it in my pocket. It was as I gave her a quick goodbye peck that she frowned and grabbed my collar.

'And don't forget to wash your neck! How on earth did you get yellow paint on it?'

Why didn't I tell her the truth there and then, tell her what had really happened? I don't know. Maybe lying was getting to be automatic. Maybe I was ashamed. I don't know. All I know is that telling her the truth simply didn't cross my mind.

'Oh, Mum, give over. I've been p-painting the layout. I must have leaned on it or something.'

Then, before she could question me further, I reached for the front-door catch and was gone.

Motto was waiting for me as I reached the park entrance where we'd been jumped the evening before. I was expecting him to want to talk about it, and he did. He pitched straight in.

'You know that refreshment hut through there? The one they only open in the summer? I bet that's where they took us.'

I hardly had time to nod my agreement or tell him I'd figured that out for myself before he went on.

'I've just been there. There's footsteps and all sorts, but you can't tell the place has been used. The padlock's still in one piece. I reckon they've got hold of a key somehow and they use it as their HQ.'

I tried to make a joke out of the memory. 'Sign on the d-door, is there? "SUN Torture Chamber"?'

'Don't knock them, Pete. What they did was justified.'

'You what?' I stopped, unable to believe I'd really heard him say it.

'What they did was justified. We've been queering their pitch. Treading on their turf. They had a right.'

'A right to b-bomb us?'

'A right to protect their turf. To warn us off. They're a team, see. We were a threat to them and they fought to deal with us. Fought *together*, Pete.'

The way he stressed the word 'together' should have warned me about the way he was thinking.

'Well I give in,' I said. 'I d-don't want to meet them again.'

'I do.'

He stepped in front of me, stopping me dead, as if he needed to make me concentrate on what he was saying. 'Can't you see, Pete?' he said. 'They're like a family...'

His voice tailed off. Then he said it. So quietly, so matter-of-fact.

'I want to join them. I want to be in a family like that.'

Shiner sits silently for a minute as he takes it in.

'That's what he said? They were his exact words?'

'N-near enough. That's why he was w-waiting for me when I arrived. He'd g-got there early. To leave a note for th-them.'

A note shoved under the door of the refreshment hut, Motto had told me. A note saying that we apologised, that we accepted we'd done wrong, that the bus depot had been SUN turf.

A note which ended by asking if we could join them.

We.

Not Motto alone, but we. Him and me. He'd never doubted that I'd want to follow him.

Shiner rubs a hand across his eyes, closes them for a few seconds. 'And neither of you knew who they were?'

'No,' I say.

He's fingering the file again, so I ask, 'D-did you?'

He flips open a page. It's a section of local street map, with crosses marked on it. He taps at them, one after another.

'Every one of those marks a SUN crew hit. Look at them. Spread out a bit, but they're mostly in one area. Their turf, right? Their circle of fame? So what do I do? Look to see what's in the centre of the circle, that's what.'

I gaze down at the bundle of crosses, the SUN crew hits. And it's there, at the centre, just as I knew it would be.

102

'Our sch-school,' I say.

'Got it in one,' says Shiner. 'Your school. I didn't know who the SUN crew were, but I was pretty sure that's where they'd be found.'

He swings the folder back and asks me, 'So, when did you find out?'

It was a couple of days later – by accident. We'd have found out one way or another, though. Motto would have made sure of that.

He was deadly serious about joining the SUN crew. After leaving his note, he talked about nothing else on the odd occasions we'd bumped into each other. Every chance he had, he went back to check out their hut. I don't know what he was expecting them to do, leave an invitation card tacked to the door or something, but there was nothing to show they'd even got his message.

That was fine by me. If they didn't come back to Motto then I wouldn't have to make my mind up about joining them. Because I hadn't made my mind up, even though Motto assumed I had.

'Pete, it'll be great. Like playing for a Premier League side!'

I wasn't so certain. Those few minutes at the bus garage, watching the SUN crew in action...they'd been frightening. Sure, we'd all been there for the same reason, doing something that would draw attention to ourselves. But the SUN crew? I got the impression it wasn't that simple for them. The depot. The Memorial Gardens. Their hit on us as well.

Their way seemed more fuelled by a blind rage than anything else.

Couldn't Motto see that? Or didn't it matter to him?

So, for once, I'd been grateful that our paths hadn't crossed for those few days.

Partly it was due to my solo lessons. They'd normally have taken place in our usual haunt, the building with the Art room upstairs, where I'd bump into Motto afterwards. Finally, though, the powers-that-be had got round to fixing the place up. When we arrived on Monday morning a high stretch of temporary fencing had already sprouted around its base. Big 'Keep Out' signs were attached to it and, behind it, men in hard hats were in the early stages of putting up scaffolding.

So it wasn't until they'd finished and the scaffolding was up that we were allowed back into the building. That's where we met up again one lunch time – and discovered who the SUN crew were.

Arriving late for afternoon registration, we'd found Mr Stowell in the open doorway of another classroom on the same floor. He was having a showdown with Terry Quarm. By the time we got there it had obviously been going on for a few minutes. Most of Quarm's year were inside the room. I spotted Jody Vahl and Lorna sitting against the near wall. In front of them, and near the door, slouched Karl Anstice.

Stowell was holding a couple of textbooks. He flicked through one to a spot he'd obviously marked.

'Your work, Quarm?'

Quarm's face didn't flicker, just registered a complete lack of concern one way or the other.

Stowell opened the other book, held them both out together. 'T-E-L,' he said, dabbing at pages that had obviously been doodled on.

'Short for telephone, sir?' called Anstice. Quarm didn't try to stifle his snigger.

'No, Anstice. Short for Terry, as in Terry Quarm.' Stowell waved the books under Quarm's nose again. 'Right or wrong?'

'Don't know, Mr Stowell.'

Stowell ploughed on, fighting a battle he must have known was hopeless, simply because he cared and those he was arguing with didn't.

'But you do know that defacing school property is against the rules, don't you, Quarm?'

Another sour voice joined the argument, from the double table beside Jody Vahl. I vaguely knew him as a heavy named Colin Upton. Next to him was a pimply lad called Aaron Byrne.

'Rules,' called Upton. 'That's all this place is.'

'True, Upton,' said Stowell. 'And take it from me, you're going to discover it doesn't get better out in the big wide world.' He turned back to Quarm. 'Now, Quarm, are you responsible for this?'

Aaron Byrne weighed in, almost as if he felt he had to now that the others had. 'Why you picking on him? Loads of kids use them books. It could have been anybody what done it.'

105

Stowell shook his head wearily. 'True, Byrne. But I just don't happen to have spotted any of the other kids doodling the same three letters on the backs of their hands during my lesson.'

Surprised, Quarm glanced down at his wrist before stupidly shoving his hands behind his back, as if the action would destroy the evidence. Then, seeing that there was no further point in arguing, denial turned to insolence.

'So? They're only History books.'

'Lower set History books,' laughed Anstice.

Stowell rounded on him. 'Not everybody can be a star, Anstice. You may be top set in most subjects but, take it from me, your attitude is rock bottom.'

Anstice didn't like that one little bit. He got to his feet, moved closer to the action. Almost as if it was a signal, the others weighed in with jibes of their own. Stowell found himself in a four-against-one argument.

'It's this dump that's rock bottom,' sneered Upton.

'Who needs school anyway?' said Byrne.

Anstice gave an imitation laugh. 'Teachers, that's who. Otherwise they'd be out on their ears.'

Mr Stowell was trying hard not to be goaded. He put a finger in the air, licked it, then made as if he was adding a score to a board.

'Very good, Anstice. Out of here with no prospect of seeing happy faces like yours ever again. How would I manage?'

'How would you waste your time, you mean.' It was

Quarm, recovering his will to fight. He scowled at Stowell. 'Because that's what you're doing here. Wasting your time and ours. All the crud you teach. It's rubbish.'

Upton again. 'Who needs it? Who needs all this junk?'

'This is just a prison. You're a jailer,' said Anstice, finger jabbing.

'And we're being kept prisoner,' spat Quarm.

Stowell looked at him. Quietly, he said, 'And you think it will be different outside, do you, Quarm?'

'Too right. We'll do what we want then.'

The teacher's eyes narrowed as he gave up any pretence of persuading or even caring.

'No you won't, you idiot. You'll still be locked in, but then it won't just be by the likes of me. It'll be by everybody you meet. They'll tie you in knots, Quarm, because they'll know more than you do.'

He moved closer, forcing Quarm to back against the wall. 'You'll still be hit by rules because there are rules out in the world too. And the fact that you're too boneheaded to understand them won't count for a thing. Whichever way you turn, you'll find yourself trapped.'

Finally Stowell snapped. Not violently, but in the worst way a basically decent man like him could manage. He made Quarm look a fool.

'You're stupid,' he said. 'Even the system will screw you. You won't be able to work out if they've given you enough unemployment money!'

Stowell's outburst hit home. The grins turned sour.

107

Shuffling, uncertain, Quarm didn't know how to fight back.

'I'm not stupid. Just because I think this place is a dump doesn't mean I'm stupid.'

'No?' snapped Stowell. 'Come on, then. What's eleven pounds ninety-five plus four pounds ninety-nine?'

In a reflex move Quarm slipped a hand into his pocket and pulled out his calculator. Stowell, forgetting himself, smacked it from his hand and sent it clattering across the floor.

'Quarm, come on. If you're not stupid you should be able to do it in your head.'

He let Quarm struggle with the sum for a couple of seconds before losing patience.

'Sixteen pounds ninety-four is the answer. The amount, Quarm, that your parents will be asked to pay to replace these books.'

That was it. Stowell stormed off down the corridor, while Quarm scowled his way across to his fallen calculator.

Motto beat him to it. Picking it up, he handed it over like he was doing a favour for a hero, his voice barely a whisper.

'I can't believe I didn't guess. You...all of you...you're the SUN crew, aren't you?'

Quarm looked over his shoulder to where Anstice was already coming out into the corridor to join him. Following him were Byrne and Upton.

'T-E-L' murmured Motto to Quarm. 'That's your tag, isn't it? And the others—'

Anstice cut him short. 'Shut it.'

The same words as Chill Voice in the hut when we were bombed. But not the same voice. There he'd tried to disguise it. That was why. In case we'd recognised it.

Motto carried on, but in a heavy whisper. 'The note. Did you get the note?'

'Shut it!' repeated Anstice.

This time, Motto did shut it. Anstice glanced at Quarm, then spun back our way as if he'd made a decision.

'So you want to join us, do you? Then be at the hut tonight. Eight sharp.'

'Four of them,' says Shiner. 'Quarm, Anstice, Byrne, Upton. Didn't it occur to you that there were always five tags with a SUN crew bombing?'

'Of c-course it did.'

CEO, ZIP, HI2U, Tel and Alpha. Tel was Quarm, we knew that. And almost the first thing that Motto said when we got to registration was that he reckoned HI2U was probably Colin Upton – like in 'Hi to Upton'.

But as to the fifth member…

'It didn't b-bother Motto,' I said. 'He reckoned the fifth one was probably some other kid they knew. Maybe someone who'd been k-kicked out of the school. There'd been a f-few.'

'So – the meeting. You went?'

I nod.

'Why?'

'Because I was t-too scared not to.'

Chapter Twelve

They were waiting for us, the four of them. No ski-masks this time, just face to face. Karl Anstice was toying with Motto's note.

'You *are* serious, then.'

Colin Upton was lounging on an old blanket, the flecks of paint on the floorboards near his feet a reminder of what they'd done to us. 'Cool, Motto,' he said, nodding. 'You've got bottle.' He turned my way. 'Both of you.'

In spite of the mickey-taking I couldn't help feeling a surge of pleasure. Motto had appreciated the compliment too. 'I want to join the SUN crew,' he said. 'No messing. I really want to.'

'I', not 'we'. A slip of the tongue, it had to be.

Terry Quarm moved to my side. 'Same goes for you does it, P-P-Pete?'

I hesitated. Did it? Did it really go for me too?

I looked at Motto, my friend. The years fell away. We were in our scrap-wood den, with eager Motto making plans, inventing schemes, cooking up fantasies, dreaming dreams of adventure and fun.

So, was this any different? Another time, another hut,

but still the same eager Motto. Motto, my friend. He wanted to join the SUN crew, didn't he? Then the same had to go for me. It couldn't go any other way.

'Sure,' I hear myself say, 'I w-want in as well.'

Anstice straightened up. 'Right. But if you want in, you've got to earn it.'

'How?' asks Motto at once.

Quarm snaps out the answer. 'We want Stowell paid back for what he did today. We want his windows trashed.'

'The building you mean? C Block?'

'No, not the building. Just his windows. The History department.'

Byrne gave a laugh, slightly nervous. 'Think of a good message to put in the middle of it, Motto. 'Stuff Stowell', something like that. Something to make him puke when he sees everybody killing themselves laughing at it.'

'Do it at the weekend,' said Quarm, relishing the thought. 'So it's there waiting on Monday.'

I hadn't expected this. 'You mean b-bust into the school?'

'No,' said Anstice.

'But the History department's up on the top floor,' said Motto. 'How else are we going to get up there?'

'Mot-to,' smiled Anstice, splitting the nickname as if it were two words, 'you want to join the crew, you've got to show you can handle it.' He looked at both of us in turn. 'You got to go up the scaffolding.'

Motto had gone pale. 'Up the scaffolding?'

112

Quarm shrugged, opened his hands. 'It's just sitting there waiting for you. Shame not to use it.'

'A few ladders to climb, that's all,' chipped in Byrne. 'No problem. Just like being a window cleaner. Except you'll be doing the opposite.'

'Making the windows dirty,' smiled Quarm.

They'd made the whole thing sound simple. Perhaps it was. I'd noticed the ladders, angled from one level of the scaffolding to the next like a fire escape, and the workmen racing up and down. We'd only have to climb up there once, do the job and get down again.

'So,' said Quarm. 'Still on are you?'

I waited for Motto to answer, willing him to back out. But all he did was lick his lips nervously.

'Because if you're not,' Upton joined in from his position on floor, 'then we have a bit of a tricky situation. You know who we are, see. You could grass on us.'

'We won't,' Motto blurted out, 'we wouldn't.'

'Well, put it this way.' Quarm circled us idly. 'Don't even think about it. Either of you...' He left the threat unspoken.

Anstice leaned forward, as if winding up a business meeting. 'Good. That's understood, then. Pass this test and you're in.'

Motto grabbed me the instant we left them.

'Pete, you've got to help me.'

He looked terrified. The only thing I could think of was that he'd lied to them. That he'd changed his mind and

113

didn't want to go through with it at all. I'd got it wrong.

'I can't go up that scaffolding,' he said.

'What?'

'I can't. No way. I'm scared of heights.'

His breathing was coming in short, sharp bursts and I could tell he wasn't joking. Then I remembered. The bus garage.

'Scared of... Is that why you didn't want to tag the roof of the K reg? Why you said I could go up there?'

He nodded. 'Yeah. I couldn't have done it. I'd have fallen off. Up high I get dizzy, see. That's what it does to me.'

'Since when?'

'I don't know. Seems like always. It even gets to me when it's safe.'

Another memory. 'Like up in the Art room?'

Even there, safe inside, he'd not wanted to get close to the windows, or stay there for long. Motto nodded. 'Makes me feel sick just looking down. If I stay there too long it all starts spinning.'

I felt like laughing. 'Scared of heights! Motto, why d-didn't you tell the SUN crew that? Why d-didn't you say so back there!'

'And have them think I'm no good? I'd have had no chance, then.' He grabbed at my shirt, pulling me close. 'Help me, Pete. Please. I'll come along, but you'll have to be the one who goes up the top. Right?'

I hesitated.

'Please! Promise me you'll do it.'

114

Motto, asking me to do something he couldn't? How could I turn him down? He'd never let me down, had he?

'I p-promise,' I said.

'Say it.'

'What?'

'Say it!'

Slowly I realised what he was talking about. And, as I said it we were kids again, back in our den.

'Cross m-my heart and hope to die,' I said.

If only I'd known...

'You agreed to go up there instead of him?' says Shiner.

All I can do is nod, show him he's getting the story straight, that the way it looked wasn't the way it happened.

It's what's led us both here, after all, sitting on opposite sides of a table with me trying to give him answers to his detective's questions – even when they're answers he doesn't want to hear.

And that one really was an answer he didn't want. He pauses for a long while as it sinks in.

'So if you agreed to climb that scaffolding for him,' he says finally, 'how come...'

The question dies on his lips, even though we both know what it was going to be.

This time, I finish the question for him as well.

'How c-come he went up there? That's what you w-want to know, isn't it?'

We're getting to the crunch. Detective Inspector Tomlinson,

115

you're going to hear exactly what happened.
    And you've got to believe me.
    What happened wasn't my fault.
    You've got to believe me.

Chapter Thirteen

After leaving Motto, I'd gone straight home. Already I was starting to regret my promise. My head was spinning, just like it had so often in school when the fruit machine was whirring its facts.

So I did what I usually did when I couldn't think straight. I went out into the garage to work on the layout.

The low-level platform was finished. The track was in place, connected and ready, diving below the ground then coming up to the surface again.

I tried a test run. Coupling three carriages to an old engine, I sent them spinning out around the circuit, then back into the new section. All went well until I brought them down to the underground platform. There, as the train reached its lowest point of travel, it snagged on a section of rail that I hadn't connected cleanly, and stopped dead.

I was just about to sort it out when Mum strolled in, looking as if she had nothing better to do.

'Have you seen the white spirit, Peter?'

The question threw me for a minute, she'd asked it so innocently. I made a point of going over to the shelf where it was kept even though I'd realised, to my horror, that I'd not returned it after cleaning off following the SUN crew's attack.

'It's not there. I've looked,' she said. 'It's not in your room, by any chance? Yellow paint on your neck and all that.'

I snatched at the opening she'd given me. 'Course, I remember now. That's wh-where it is. I'll get it.'

'No hurry.' She moved closer, looking over the layout. 'So where's the bit you've been painting yellow?'

As I recalled my hasty answer to Mum when she'd ragged me about the yellow paint on my neck, I realised how stupid I'd been to say I'd done it while working on the layout. None of my changes were in that colour. I tried to backtrack.

'Then it must have happened at sch-school. During Art.'

'I didn't notice it over the weekend. Only on Monday morning. Working on your Art project with Mark at the weekend, were you?'

'Right. That must have been it.'

Mum fixed me with a steady gaze. 'You said it was a Geography project.'

'No. Art.'

'It was Art the first time you mentioned it. Last time it was Geography. It's back to Art again now, is it?'

I was getting flustered and it began to show. 'D-does it matter? So I g-got some paint on me. What's the big deal?'

She said nothing for maybe twenty seconds, as if she was

118

weighing up what she should say next. When she did speak, I felt it with the force of a thunderbolt.

'The big deal is that you're lying, and have been all along. I'm right, aren't I.' It was a statement, not a question.

I shouted, as if that would help convince her. 'I'm not lying! Look, I g-got some paint on me. I d-don't know where it came from. End of story, Mum.'

She nudged open the garage door and picked up the carrier bag she'd left on the ground outside.

'No it isn't the end of the story, Peter. It's just the beginning.'

She still hadn't raised her voice. That's what was really unnerving me.

Mum had always been more excitable; Dad the calm one. Yet here she was, acting just like him. She didn't raise her voice, even when she dropped the bag into my hands and asked, 'What happened to this lot?'

I looked blankly down at the bag I'd dumped in the bin after the SUN crew hit us. My paint-sodden clothes were still inside, but now stiff and hard where the paint had dried.

'You made the mistake of hiding them under a newspaper I hadn't read,' she said. 'Otherwise I might not have found them. So, I'll ask you again. What happened to them, Peter?'

Still I tried to fob her off with a story.

'OK. It was just a stupid g-game. A couple of the kids at

school brought spray cans in. We all started m-messing about but it got out of hand and turned into a f-fight. I threw them away because I knew you'd g-go spare if you saw them.'

'Peter, don't lie to me!' This time there was steel in her voice. 'That's your best shirt in there, not a school one.'

She pulled it out, holding it by the cuffs so that the full mess of trash and SUN crew tags were clear to see.

'Do you think I don't know what this lot is? I work for a cleaning business, or had you forgotten! What do you think I do? It's not all vacuum cleaning, you know! I spend plenty of my time cleaning this sort of muck off walls and floors and God knows where else!'

She jabbed an angry finger back and forth, picking out the tags. 'SUN. CEO. ZIP. HI2U. Tel. They're – what do they call them – tags, aren't they?'

My head felt like it had a whirlpool inside it. I didn't want to tell her, but she wasn't going to budge until I did – enough of it to satisfy her, anyway.

'OK. They j-jumped us. Motto and me. On our w-way home from the cinema.'

'Who jumped you?'

'Them.' I pointed at the SUN tag, sprayed across my shirt. 'They're called the SUN c-crew.'

'Why didn't you tell me?'

'B-because…because I didn't want you to worry.'

'Who are they? Did you recognise them?'

'No. They all had m-masks on.'

For a moment she seemed satisfied. But then she looked again at the shirt, at the SUN crew tags.

'Why did they do it?' she asked.

The question threw me. I shrugged, tried to bluff it out. 'I d-don't know. Why do they do anything?'

'I don't know why they put graffiti on buildings and the like,' said Mum. 'That's beyond me. But attacking people? I think I can guess why they do that. Because they've got a score to settle.'

'What?'

She was like a hound on the scent, and there was no way she was going to let go. 'Are you one, Peter? A graffiti vandal?'

'No!'

'Did you and Mark get on the wrong side of these thugs? Is that why they did this?'

'No! No I t-tell you!'

She looked me square in the eye. 'Are you into graffiti. Yes or no?'

'N-n-no.' I could barely force the word out.

'Promise?'

'I...promise.'

She nodded, once. 'All right. I believe you.'

Turning on her heel, she went back into the house. On the way she dropped the carrier bag back into the bin without a second look.

Had she believed me? I couldn't tell. But the fact was that I'd lied to her again and I hated myself for it.

121

On the layout my test train was still whining gently, stuck on the badly connected track in my underground section – my test train, that had happily rattled around for years on the surface but had now been sent on a new route and got stuck in the darkness.

And as I bent to release it I couldn't escape one thought.

That train was me.

I suppose what I'm saying is that, even as I packed some spray cans in my rucksack and tucked it out of sight in the garage, I was having doubts.

I felt like I was walking along a see-saw and had come to the point in the middle.

One side there was Motto, and what he seemed so keen on – continuing the graf and, especially, getting in with the SUN crew.

On the other side, there was – what? No Motto? That was the difficult bit to handle. I'd always been at his end of the see-saw, no question. But now the balance was shifting.

For twenty-four hours I didn't know what to do. Then something happened which tipped the balance completely. And it was Motto himself who did it.

I'd spent Saturday morning working on the layout. It was almost done. By eleven o'clock I'd just got some making good to do, sticking back some figures and small items that I'd had to prise off to give me access to the baseboard, and that would be it. It was then, as I gathered together the things I needed, that I discovered I'd run out of modelling cement.

The only shop that sold decent stuff was in town. I headed off, and was ambling back through the arcade, when I saw him ahead of me. I caught him up just as he was going into the sports shop.

Maybe if I'd noticed the signs in the window I'd have realised why. As it was, I just followed him in.

'Looking for anything special?' I said.

'Just mooching. Here, do us a favour and hang on to this. I just want to nip upstairs and see what they've got.'

He handed me the bag he was holding and strode off. Not being any the wiser, I just had a wander around until he came down again. I heard the bag I was holding for him rustle, but he didn't take it back.

Then, saying, 'Nah. They haven't got any,' in a voice loud enough for the shop assistant to hear, he edged me towards the door.

It was as we went through it that all hell seemed to break loose.

One minute Motto was beside me. The next, a high-pitched alarm started wailing and he was snatching his bag from my fingers and yelling, 'Run!'

For a moment I was flummoxed. I looked round. Inside the shop a guy wearing a white shirt and a badge was already on the move and heading our way. Only then did I twig to what he'd done.

It was almost too late. With a sudden spurt the white-shirted guy grabbed at my arm. Wrenching myself free, I careered down the street after Motto. Ducking across the road, I followed him through a maze of alleys, my heart pounding until finally we were running up the path to his house and I knew we'd got safely away.

Only then did I discover what it had all been about. Flopping on to his bed, flushed with pleasure, Motto dipped a hand into the bag he'd asked me to hold – and pulled out the black ski-mask he'd stolen.

'Black ski-mask.' Shiner sighs as he says it. 'As worn by the SUN crew.'

'Yeah. As worn b-by the SUN crew.'

Leaning back on my seat, I gaze up at the bare ceiling. A small corner of my mind is asking why places like this have to look so miserable, but right at the front it's remembering how the full meaning of what he'd done had slowly sunk in...

'Look at this,' breathed Motto. He slipped the mask over his head. The plastic security tag was still on it. 'Cool, or what?'

The rustle of the bag in the shop. He'd slid that mask into it while I was holding it for him. And let me carry it out of the shop.

'That was a st-stupid thing to do!' I shouted.

He pulled the mask off. 'What's your problem? Didn't get caught, did you?'

'No thanks to you! I w-was holding that bag!'

Motto spread his hands. 'Pete, it was spur of the moment stuff. Didn't you see the sign in the window?'

'What sign?'

'Winter sports gear. They'd just got their new stock in.'

He held up the ski-mask as if it was a trophy. He was totally unconcerned. He just didn't see what I was on about. All he could do was sit there cradling that mask.

'I was n-nearly caught!'

'OK, kid. So it was a bit hairy. But the risk was worth it.'

For a second my stutter seemed to take over complete control of my tongue. 'N-n-not for m-me it w-wasn't!'

Motto's face flashed a look I'd never seen before. Correction. It flashed a look I'd had plenty of times from other kids, but never from him. Never from my best friend.

'You want one too, is that it?' he sneered. 'All right, P-P-Pete, I'll go back and nick one for you later.'

Never, never before, had he made fun of me like that.

For the first time in my life I felt like punching him, lashing out at him, hurting him in any way I could.

'I d-don't want one!' I shouted. 'I couldn't care less about the SUN crew!'

He simply shrugged.

Leaning across to his bedside table, he pulled out a sheet of paper. He'd been practising. The message 'Stuff Stowell' had been laid out on it, exactly as he planned it to go up on the school windows. With a black felt-tip he began to etch in some extra detail.

'See you tomorrow then,' he said, not even looking up.

125

'No way.'

The words felt as if they'd come from another person, even though I knew they'd come from me. This time Motto did look up.

'What?'

There was no ducking it. 'Like I said. No way. I'm not doing it.'

He changed tack then, trying to make me laugh, thrusting his hand into the ski-mask and poking his fingers out through the eye-holes. 'Hey. I'm sorry, right? I should have told you what I was up to.'

When I didn't react, he tried a Motto-ism. 'Come on, Pete. Think about it. Tomorrow's going to be great. We'll do such a brilliant job on those windows they'll have to change their tag to the SUNNIER crew when we join them.'

I got up, reached for the door. 'Forget it, Motto. You d-don't need me.'

In an instant, his mood switched again. Leaping in front of me he barred my way. 'You've got to do it. Got to!'

'Give me one good reason.'

'One? I can give you five. The SUN crew. You heard what they said. If we don't do it they'll be after us, and this time it won't just be a paint-balling.'

'We? M-me, you mean. They won't be after you, Motto. You're one of them already. You've even got the right headgear.'

I heaved his arm aside and swung open the door to his

126

room. Struggling back, trying to push it closed again, he made a last desperate attempt to stop me leaving.

'You promised! Cross your heart and hope to die!'

I said nothing. Levering his bedroom door open, I forced my way past him and out on to the landing. He followed me, still pleading.

'Pete, come on! You've got to come with me. We're partners aren't we?'

I stopped, stood there at the top of the stairs just like I'd been standing there and seen his mother slap his sister's face. What had Lorna said to me that day? 'He likes you around because you make him look good.'

Motto gripped my shoulders. 'We're partners,' he repeated. 'Always have been, right? Well if you're my partner you'll come with me.'

'Forget it, Motto. I've never been your p-partner. Just your android.'

I walked away from him then.

For the first time in my life I walked down the stairs, away from Motto.

Behind me, he ranted on. 'Stuff you, then! I'll do it myself. I don't need you, P-P-Pete. Get that? I don't need you!'

He thundered down the stairs behind me. I kept on going, up the path and out into the street we'd played in so often.

Hearing the front door slam shut behind me, I couldn't help myself. I glanced back. At one of the upstairs windows I saw a curtain twitch.

But it wasn't Motto's face that appeared briefly.

It was Lorna's.

'Lorna knew what was going on, then?' asks Shiner.

'Definitely. She was only across the l-landing. She must have heard it all.'

He gets to his feet, paces up and down as he tries to fit the pieces together. He's wasting his time. Only I know how they all fit together, and he's going to find out soon enough now.

'She couldn't have t-talked him out of it, you know. No chance. Even if she'd told him everything.'

'Could anybody have talked him out of it?' says Shiner.

'I was going to try,' I say.

It's true. After storming out I'd retreated to the garage as usual and, as I worked on the layout, tried to think it through. I couldn't – OK, wouldn't – believe that for Motto and me it was all over.

By the time Sunday evening arrived and the clock was moving round towards the time I knew he'd be going out, I'd decided that I had to try again.

'Why?' asks Shiner.

I shrug. 'Because...' There's only one image I can think of that will explain it to him. 'Because my t-train had come out of the tunnel. His was still down there.'

'So you went to the house?'

I nod. 'There was n-nobody at home, though. No Motto, no

Lorna...nobody.'

Shiner sits down opposite me again, his eyes fixed on mine. We're nearly there. It's the moment he's been waiting for.

'So you went to the school?'

'Yeah. I w-went to the school.'

Chapter Fourteen

I'd climbed over the fence and run across the school grounds, crouching as though I'd just got out of a helicopter. The sun was about as low as it could get, turning my shadow into a long streak as I ran. Ahead of me I could see the scaffolding, clinging to C Block like poison ivy.

High up, the dying rays of the sun were bouncing off the school windows, painting them a fiery red. That's why I couldn't tell if anything had been done to them until I was virtually there. Then, looking up, I saw they were still clear.

Had I got it wrong? Hadn't Motto arrived yet? Had he gone somewhere else? Or had he had second thoughts, in spite of what he'd said?

If so, then somebody else must have been there. As I looked around, I saw that the gate leading through the builders' security fence wasn't shut but was swinging back and forth in the light breeze.

Moving closer I saw the padlock on the ground, its clasp bent and twisted. Then, near by, something else, something black, in with the builders' rubble.

Motto's stolen ski-mask.

That was when I heard it, coming from high above me, an awful whispering kind of shout.

'Help! Help me!'

Stepping back, I looked up in the direction of the cry, this time letting my eye move more slowly along the top level.

Motto was there.

As the final few rays of the sun bounced off the school windows, I saw him silhouetted against the deep red. He was on his knees, holding on to a scaffolding upright as he cowered in fear. Realising that I'd spotted him, he cried out again, louder this time.

'Pete! Help. For God's sake.'

I shielded my eyes, trying to focus on him better. 'You OK?' I called.

For a moment he didn't answer, as if he was trying to decide if it was safe for him to open his mouth.

'Can't get down,' he managed finally. 'I'm – too – scared.'

Of course. What had he said? *I can't go up that scaffolding. I'm scared of heights.*

He'd wanted me to do it for him, but I'd walked out. So he'd tried to do it himself and it had all gone wrong.

Even from where I was, I could hear him breathing heavily, gulping in air as he tried to contain the panic that was just below the surface. I tried to calm him, even though I felt anything but calm myself.

'Motto. T-take it easy. Just climb down s-slowly.'

His response, almost a cry, came back at once. 'No ladder…'

What was he on about? I looked to my right. The base of the lowest ladder was in touching distance, leading up from the ground to the first level. From there, other ladders zig-zagged upwards from one level to the next.

Didn't they?

I took a step back and checked the rest of the scaffolding tower. The ladder from the first level to the second was in place. Angled from left to right, its top jutted through a gap in the scaffolding boards by a good metre and a half. Another ladder, further along the second level, led up to the third in the same way.

It was only when I looked for the one which should have led from the third level up to where Motto was crouching that I realised what he was saying. That ladder was nowhere to be seen.

It had to have fallen down. Motto, shaking like a leaf, must have dislodged it somehow. It had to be lying there, up on the third level. I could put it back in place if I climbed up there.

'I'm coming up,' I called.

Stuffing the ski-mask in my pocket, I ran to the foot of the ground-level ladder and began to climb. With every step I took the whole structure seemed to shake. The five metres to the first level seemed like fifty. Carefully I stepped off the ladder and on to the whitewash-dotted scaffolding boards.

The gentle breeze I'd felt down at the bottom seemed to have picked up strength, making the scaffolding sing as it whistled through it. Slowly I made my way along to the next ladder and started up that. Every rung seemed to shake beneath my feet, seemed to make it wobble from side to side. I tried not to take my eyes off the next rung, tried not to look to the side and through the windows to the classrooms with their empty chairs and ghostly books left on the tables.

Reaching the second level I called, 'Motto. How you doing?' His answer was wordless, a frightened groan.

I walked gingerly along the planking. The next zig-zag ladder would get me to the third level. There I'd see what had happened, put it right, help Motto down.

I put my foot on the bottom rung and started climbing – higher, higher, up towards the gap in the planking above my head, the ladder swaying like a rolling ship. I reached the gap, my head, my waist, passing through it as though I was climbing up into an attic, then kept on going until I'd reached the top of the ladder and was able to step sideways on to the third level.

'N-nearly there, Motto.'

I could see him now, immediately above my head, through the gaps of the top level's planking. I could see his rucksack, and the spray cans he'd unloaded. But it was Motto I was concerned about. Even from where I was I could see he was shaking with fear, his arms, his legs, his whole body making the scaffolding boards rattle.

'I'm just going to sort out the ladder,' I said. 'I'll be up there with you in a tick.'

'Thanks. Thanks, Pete. You're the best mate anyone could have.'

I was trying to sound confident, but I wasn't feeling it. Hauling the ladder back into place wasn't going to be easy. That high up, I felt as though I needed four hands – two to lift the ladder and another two to hang on to the scaffolding so as to stop myself falling off. Turning, I looked along the level to where the ladder should be.

It wasn't there.

What's more, it hadn't simply slipped down; it had fallen away from where it should be and gone over the side of the scaffolding.

I saw it then. It was far below, buried so deeply in the shrubbery close to the base of the structure that it would have been impossible for me to spot when I was down at ground level. And it looked to be hopelessly bust.

I told him the bad news as calmly as I could.

'The ladder's g-gone, Motto. It's fallen right down to the ground. I think it's b-bust.'

'It can't have.' Motto's voice was barely under control. 'Pete, you've got to help me. I've got to get down!'

'How did it happen?'

'I don't know. I climbed up – God, I was scared. I was getting the stuff out when I heard it go. I didn't know what had happened. I just stayed put. Maybe fifteen minutes. Then I heard you come.'

It was the real Motto speaking. No funnies, no strutting, just another kid as lost as me. But he'd sounded calmer, so

135

I tried the only answer I could think of.

'I'll go down again, Motto. I'll g-get help.'

'No! Don't leave me!'

'It's the only way.'

'No!' he yelled again, gaining the strength to shout. He wouldn't move, but he didn't want me to move either.

It was the far-off wail of a siren that broke the deadlock.

'It must be the police,' he moaned. 'They're coming!'

Suddenly, as if he was more scared of getting caught than he was of the height, the scaffolding boards above my head began to rock. Through the gaps I could see that Motto was struggling to his feet although not loosening his grip on the upright he was holding. His legs hardly looked strong enough to support him.

'What are you doing?' I cried.

He didn't answer. Having got to his feet he'd edged his way to the gap in the boarding where the ladder had been. It was right on the outer edge of the scaffolding, presumably so that workers wouldn't step back and accidentally fall through it. As he reached it he slipped to his knees again, then on to his stomach so that he was lying flat with his toes towards the gap.

I saw him peer out, as if he was looking over the edge of a cliff. He shuddered, closed his eyes, and pulled his head back in. I looked down too then, at the shrubbery and the rubble-strewn area inside the chain-link fence. The sight made me feel giddy. I could only imagine what it had done to Motto.

Then I heard the squeak of a trainer on metal. I looked up. Motto, still on his stomach, had twisted himself round. Still holding an upright of the scaffolding he was wriggling backwards so as to push his feet and ankles through the gap in the planking where the ladder should have been. He was still too far above me to reach.

'Motto! B-be careful!'

I could hear his laboured breathing as he slowly pushed his legs out into space. I could see what he wanted to do. By letting himself down he could loop his legs round the scaffolding upright below the planking and slide down to my level as if it was a rope exercise in the gym. Trouble was, he'd only pushed his legs out as far as the top of his shins then stopped at that. He was going to have to screw up the courage to let them out far enough to dangle.

'Back further, Motto,' I called. 'But be c-careful.'

'I can't,' cried Motto, 'I'll fall.'

I tried to be encouraging. I wish now I'd been the opposite, tried telling him he had no chance and made him go back.

Or am I kidding myself? I think I am. It wouldn't have changed anything. He was committed. It had just been a case of him screwing up the courage. Or of something forcing him to do it.

The next wail of the police car's siren, much nearer this time, did just that.

'They're coming!' he cried.

Panic-stricken, he started wriggling backwards. I saw his

thighs emerge, and then suddenly he was bent over the planking like a rag doll on a bed, his feet waving frantically from side to side as they tried to locate the scaffolding pole he was after.

That was when he slipped.

'Motto!'

Even as I shouted, he gave a cry of fear. He needed my help and I couldn't reach him. I could see he was trying to regain his grip by levering himself up again. But all that did was make things worse. His legs began to flail – and I couldn't do a thing to help.

All I could do was to scream at him, 'Hold on! Hold on!'…until, in that one terrible moment, I heard the clatter and saw him lose his grip.

I touched him as he fell.

I saw the look of terror on his face, his mouth open in a silent scream, and our fingers touched as he went past me. Then he was arching backwards, falling through space.

I turned away, buried my face in my hands, heard the dull thump as he ploughed into the shrubbery below.

I couldn't look down. Racing back, ignoring the thundering planks beneath my feet, ignoring the ladders as they juddered, ignoring the siren coming closer then dying with a moan very near by, ignoring the men leaping out and running my way, I made it to ground level.

'Motto!' I screamed blindly, diving off the bottom ladder.

I ran straight into Shiner.

I saw the terrible look on his face as, in the same instant

as me, we both realised the full horror of what had happened.

Framed in the bushes, Motto was lying on his back like a fractured star – lying next to the ladder that would have saved him.

He wasn't making a sound. He wasn't moving.

And then Shiner was over there with him, weeping like a baby, crying hot tears as he looked down on his son's broken body.

Chapter Fifteen

Shiner buries his head in his hands at the memory.

'Shiner' – the silly name I'd given him after first seeing him in the front room of his house not long after Motto and I had first bumped into each other, in the days when he was plain PC Bryan Tomlinson.

I can only imagine what's going through his mind. If it's anything like mine, it's weird, a kind of crystal-clear blur.

The running footsteps; the patrol-car driver barking instructions into his radio; more lights and sirens as the ambulance screeched up; Motto being encased in some sort of bubble affair before being laid on a stretcher with infinite care and then driven away: they're the blurs.

But what Motto looked like, lying there – that's the crystal-clear part. Try as I might I can't get that to blur over at all.

'Somebody rang in to the Unit and said there were two kids on the scaffolding. I was there to take the call.'

Shiner wipes the back of his hand across his eyes. 'Story of my life. Always there to take the call, that was me. Job first, everything else last.' He corrects himself. 'Everybody else last, more like. Including my own kids.'

'Motto w-wanted to see more of you. They both did. Him and L-Lorna.'

'I know that now. When you said about him wanting to join that crew...be in a family...'

He gets up, walks away for a minute, stares blankly out of the window. The talk of family has got to him.

It's got to me, too.

*As he comes back to sit opposite me again I'm thinking of my family. Mum **and** Dad.*

I glance to my side. Mum's as motionless as a statue, staring straight in front of her.

Is she thinking of what she did? I wonder.

Of what she did in Dad's name?

They put me in the back of the patrol car. From there I saw the ambulance arrive and Motto being transferred to it like he was a piece of china. I saw Shiner go with him.

There followed a short drive for me. Then out, up some steps, and into a drab interview room in the police station. Mum had been called. She was already there, her eyes red as if she'd been crying for a while. I caught odd words as my escort spoke to her briefly.

'Known graffiti vandal. And his friend. Fall. Intensive care.'

Then I was sat down at a table, Mum next to me, the policeman opposite, to go through what had happened.

After, Mum was allowed to drive me home. We sat in

silence all the way. When we got there she led me into our cramped front room where she rang the hospital. As she put the phone down I feared the worst.

'M-Motto. He's not...'

'Dead? No. But he's got a fractured skull and internal injuries. If he does live there's the chance he might have brain damage. Right now, he's in a coma.'

Suddenly she cracked. 'What were you doing there! Tell me!'

It's as if none of what I'd said at the police station had sunk in. So I went through it again in short, sharp detail – the raids, the tagging, the lies I'd told her. All of it. Afterwards we sat there in silence for some while.

Then, suddenly, she stood up. 'Come with me.'

I followed her out through the back door and down to the garage. Flicking on the humming, fluorescent light, we went inside.

My rucksack – the rucksack I'd used on the depot raid with Motto – was just inside the door.

'Yours, I take it?' she said, picking it up. 'You didn't hide it very well. It took me about two minutes to find it after the police called.'

I nodded. There was no point in denying it. 'I was going to g-go on the raid with Motto. B-but I changed my mind. I wanted to talk him out of it.'

She opened the rucksack and lifted out one of the spray cans inside. 'Why should I believe you, Peter?'

'It's true!'

Almost idly, she took the cap off the canister, turning it round in her hand as she spoke.

'Your dad hated people like you, do you know that?'

I looked at her, not understanding.

'He'd come home after driving a train that had been attacked by people like you and he'd have tears in his eyes at the stupidity of it all. Because that's what it is, Peter. Stupid and destructive. If he was here he'd have told you that.'

It was as if she'd torn at an open wound. 'Well he's not here, is he!' I shouted.

Once again, just like the previous time we'd argued, she did a Dad on me and spoke slowly and quietly.

'No, he's not. But I am. And I'm telling you what he'd have told you. That people like you have got to be stopped.'

Her coolness brought me back to my senses. 'I have stopped, Mum. I'm f-finished with it. You've got to believe me.'

'I'd like to believe you, Peter. Like I told myself I should believe you when you promised me you weren't involved in it. But – I just don't think I can.'

Her index finger was dabbing lightly at the white button on top of the spray can. 'The trouble is, there's not much I can do if you decide to start again. Except...'

She paused, then looked me in the eye so that I got the full impact of what she'd steeled herself to say.

'...except teach you what it's like to be on the receiving end of people like you.'

And then slowly, deliberately, she aimed the spray can down at the layout.

It was as if I was in a terrible dream. I heard the hiss of the spray. I saw the jet of paint splatter across the underground platform I'd been working on for so long. I couldn't believe it was happening.

Only when she speeded up, spraying again in a wide arc that seared across the buildings and track that Dad had spent years making, did what she was doing finally sink in.

'Stop it!'

She didn't take any notice. She just continued to spray paint along the length of the layout, faster and faster, making circles, squiggles, shapes.

'Stop it! Stop it!'

I was screaming by then. I lunged across to try and snatch the can from her, but she held me off as she continued bombing what both Dad and I had put our hearts and souls into for so long.

I shouted. I screamed. It did no good.

Still she went on, covering my lettering and markings with swathes of paint. I struggled with her again and again, the hissing of the spray can sounding in my ears like a pounding headache, until all I could do was give up the fight and crumple into a crying heap on the floor.

Finally the can was exhausted. She came to me then, bent down beside me.

'Why? Why?' I screamed the words, hardly recognising

the sound of my own voice, so thick with pain. 'Why did you have to do that?'

She answered slowly, as if she was having trouble saying the words. 'So that now you know.'

I looked up at her then, hating her.

She stood up, her shoulders slumping as she let the spray can fall from her fingers to land with a clatter on the concrete floor. Only then did I notice the tears coursing down her own cheeks.

Slowly she walked over to the notice board and looked up at Dad's faded photograph pinned there.

'I'm sorry, love,' she whispered. 'I'm so sorry.'

And she began to sob like a baby.

Shiner sits down opposite me again, now. He glances at Mum, then back to me. We're all feeling it, I guess. It's not much fun being honest.

There's more to come, though, we both know that. The story didn't end with Motto.

'You didn't believe me, did you?' I say. 'When I t-told you I'd only gone there to try and talk Motto out of it.'

'No. Would you?'

I shrug. 'Suppose not. But I t-told you why. I told you about the SUN crew, who they were. D-didn't that make a difference?'

He opens the folder again, checks the handwritten notes, nods. 'It helped. We sent a detective in to have a chat with your Mr Stowell. That's when he mentioned the business of the graffiti on the book.'

'Qu-Quarm? T-E-L?'

'Right. So we told him who we thought they were and asked him to keep us posted if he saw or heard anything.'

'But you didn't g-go for the SUN crew.'

'Not straight away, no,' says Shiner. 'Even if they had been behind what happened at the school, there was nothing to link them with it. Besides, I preferred them to think they weren't under suspicion.'

'I d-didn't know that.'

For the first time, I see him give a flicker of a smile. 'Now that I do believe.'

First thing Monday morning I was excluded from school. No surprise, I suppose, what with the facts being the way they were. On its own the fact that I'd admitted being on the scaffolding with Motto would have been sufficient. But as the rest of the evidence – that he'd been planning to tag the school windows – couldn't be disputed either, that was that. Mum couldn't argue with the decision, and didn't.

A couple of days passed. Neither of us spoke much. Mum went to work and came home as usual but, whatever time she got in, always rang the hospital straight away.

'No change,' she'd say dully. 'He's still very bad. Still in a coma.'

As for me, I forced myself out to the garage to see the damage she'd done to the layout. Staring at it, I grew angrier and angrier. Angry at myself. Angry, so angry, at her.

147

Angry at Motto for falling, even.

Time and again I ran the accident through in my mind, turning the clock back in the only way possible, wondering if I could have done more to help him.

If, if, if...

I'd felt I was at the deepest part of the tunnel before, but that was nothing to the way I felt now.

It seemed to me I'd lost everything.

Dad.

Motto.

Mum, even, after all that had happened.

I felt the rage burning inside me and lashed out with my foot, sending a black lump of cloth flying across the floor. As it landed I realised what it was: Motto's stolen black ski-mask. It must have fallen out of my pocket when I'd slumped there during Mum's rampage.

I picked it up, twisting it in my hands while I inspected the ruined layout – ruined, just like Motto's life.

As the fury bubbled inside me I looked down at the ski-mask in my hands. I must have stared at that mask for a good five minutes, trying to work out what it all meant.

Finally, the fruit machine stopped spinning. The barrels clicked into place. And, for once, they gave me a combination I could understand.

At that moment, I knew what I had to do.

I had to hit back.

*

It didn't take me long to realise that the SUN crew hadn't been turned over by Shiner or his people. They weren't taking any special precautions.

Posting myself near the hut in the park, I saw Karl Anstice and Terry Quarm pick the lock and go inside. Not long after, Colin Upton arrived and joined them.

Three down, two to go.

I shrank back into the trees as, ten minutes later, Aaron Byrne turned up. A quick rattle on the door, a few muffled calls of welcome, and he went inside.

One to go.

I hung on, checking my watch, until I couldn't afford to wait any longer. Hurrying across to the hut I put my ear to the door, heard a couple of laughs, then the sound of all four of them moving towards the door.

I opened it and stepped inside.

I had the advantage of surprise, as I'd hoped. Suspecting they'd jump me and ask questions later, I knew exactly what I was going to say.

'I've got a proposal to make. A b-bombing raid.'

They glanced at each other, doubt in their faces, not knowing what to make of me. I kept talking.

'I want to do it for M-Motto,' I spat. 'Hit them for his sake. B-bomb them for him.'

Further looks at each other, but more relaxed this time as they saw I was alone. A look of amusement crossed Quarm's face. The others saw it and followed suit.

It was Karl Anstice who spoke first, mockingly. 'Get

149

stuffed, toy.'

'Hear me out.'

'You what? You're jinxed. Motto's in hospital because of you.'

Byrne moved towards me, copying Anstice. 'We don't want jinxes in our crew, toy.'

'Listen!' I pleaded. 'Where I'm thinking of you haven't b-bombed before. Nobody has.'

'There are plenty of places we haven't hit,' said Anstice. 'It's a big town. We'll get round to them all in good time, though.'

He smiled at the others, got a round of grins back again, all amused together. I had to get them to take me seriously. It was risky.

'I reckon there's another r-reason you haven't hit the p-place I'm thinking of.'

Quarm's eyes flickered. 'Which is?'

'You're all chicken.'

I'd hit home. Quarm clenched his fists. Upton and Byrne scowled. Only Anstice kept his look of mild amusement. Or tried to. I noticed a small muscle twitching at the side of his temple as he said, 'I don't think you mean that, P-P-Pete.'

'I do,' I said. 'I reckon you haven't hit this place b-because it's too much.'

'What place?' snapped Quarm, unable to stop himself. 'Where are you talking about?'

I'd got them. Got their attention. I glanced from one to

150

the other before answering.

'Ripple Lane Sidings,' I said finally.

More glances, this time accompanied by small gasps of surprise – and fear. A sure sign that they were seeing the place in their minds.

I'd had the idea in the garage, as I'd turned the ski-mask over in my hands and looked across at my splattered, ruined layout. Ripple Lane Sidings were part of that layout, had been the hardest part of all for Dad to get right.

They're situated half a kilometre east of Longbridge Station, where the electrified line splits into fingers like a skeleton's hand. Tube trains from the City can be parked there overnight, saving them the trek on through to the Upminster terminus, another half-hour at least. Ripple Lane Sidings had the capacity to hold at least ten six-car trains.

'We've done trains before,' scoffed Anstice.

I had my argument all ready. 'Inside, sure. Late at night, empty carriages where n-nobody can see you. I'm talking about t-tagging the outsides.'

'We've t-tagged outsides,' said Byrne, mimicking again.

'Quick tags when the train pulls into the station,' I said, doing my best to make it sound trivial. 'What I'm talking about is different league. I'm talking about a complete blitz. Like at the bus d-depot. For that you need time and space.'

A pause. 'Go on,' said Anstice. The muscle was still twitching.

'That means hitting them at night, while they're in the

151

s-sidings. There could be ten in there, easy.'

'What about security?' said Quarm. 'We're not mugs, toy. Only mugs walk into heavily guarded places.'

He's looking for a way out, I'm sure of it. That's when I hit them with the argument I hope they can't beat.

'Sure there's security,' I sneered. 'But I know how to beat it. B-because I know all there is to know about that place, don't I?'

Byrne turned to the others. 'His dad used to work there. As a train driver.'

Anstice swung round on him sharply. 'Quick thinking,' he said sarcastically. 'Very zippy, ZIP. Tell us something we don't know.'

ZIP, one of the crew's solo tags. It has to be Byrne's.

'Ask me,' I said. 'I can tell you what you d-don't know. That is, if you want to know.'

Again they exchange glances, getting irritated with each other. They don't fancy it, that's clear. But Quarm, for one, is trying not to show it.

'How about cameras?' he asked. 'They've got cameras haven't they?'

'Only at the st-station end. They haven't been extended to the far end yet. We could come in from that d-direction and they'd never spot us.'

They're looking at each other now, uncertain.

'I can lead you in,' I go on. 'I can g-give you everything: plans, diagrams, the lot. All except for one thing. I can't give you the b-bottle. The guts.'

It's my 'chicken' jibe again. This time I have to wait for an answer as Quarm, Byrne and Upton look at Anstice. I realise then that, out of the four of them, he's the one in charge.

And he's worried. The muscle's twitching. A bead of sweat creeps out from beneath his hairline.

'You saying we haven't got it?' he says finally.

'I don't have to say it. If you've g-got the bottle, then you'll do it.'

Byrne gave a little laugh. 'What's the big deal, guys? They turn the electricity off at night, don't they?'

I laugh at him. 'Of course they d-don't. That's why it needs bottle!'

He can't take his eyes off me as I go on. I don't know where I get it from, but the words are coming like they never have before. I'm winding them up, testing them.

'Step on a live rail and you'll have six hundred and thirty volts g-going through you. That's what it takes to p-power a train. Get a belt like that – it's curtains. Your heart will stop in an instant. Or, if you're unlucky, m-maybe a little longer than an instant. Long enough for you to know what's happening. Maybe even long enough to smell yourself b-burning.'

I turned back to Anstice, staring him out as the other three waited. That's when he asked the question I'd been expecting all along.

'Why? Why do you want to do it?'

'Why do you think?' I snapped. 'To get my own back.

They took my d-dad from me. I hate them. What have I g-got to lose?'

Before he had a chance to answer, I nailed him. I looked around at them all, but I was talking to Anstice. 'So, are you in? Or d-do I hit them on my own and put it about that the SUN c-crew didn't have the guts to come with me?'

Anstice hesitated. 'When?'

I answered at once. I'd thought it through completely. Maybe it was a fluke, maybe not, but for once I felt as if the fruit machine had given me a winning combination.

'Sunday night,' I said. 'That's when the s-sidings are full, all ready for the Monday rush. We can b-bomb the lot, ten at least, maybe more.'

One more hesitation, one more flicker of doubt. Then his mind was made up.

'Where?' he said.

'Meet me at Ripple Lane. Under the f-footbridge. Midnight.'

Anstice looked up at me then, his lips twitching into a hard smile. 'We'll be there, P-P-Pete. All five of us.'

Chapter Sixteen

I had things to get ready.

Out in the garage I studied the devastated layout, committing every scrap of it to memory. By the time Sunday came, I knew the location of every cable run, every junction box, every signal, every floodlight.

More importantly, I knew every inch of track. The up and down main lines, adjoining each other, their overhead power systems high above them. Beside them the electrified underground lines, the one to Upminster next door to the main lines, the down line to Longbridge and the City on the far side. And, in between these two electrified lines, the maze of points and splintering which were the Ripple Lane Sidings.

These I drew out time and time again until I could do it automatically, seeing in my mind's eye how and where the fingers of track formed and ran.

I could see from the model exactly where I would lead them in. The footbridge where I'd told them to meet me crossed the line at the rear of Longbridge Hospital, beyond the eastern tip of the sidings. There, as Dad's layout showed, only a low brick wall separated the pavement from the sloping embankment dropping down towards the tracks. Over that simple wall and it would be no more than a four hundred metre walk alongside the main line track to the sidings themselves.

And, there, my fight back would take place.

For the umpteenth time, I turned the ski-mask over in my hands. Again I saw myself picking it up from where I'd first seen it, down at the foot of the scaffolding, with Motto shaking with fear high above.

Motto's stolen ski-mask – or so I'd thought until I'd kicked at it in the garage and then looked at it again.

Looked at it properly, and seen that it wasn't the mask that Motto had stolen at all. It couldn't have been.

For on the back of this one a symbol had been clearly marked.

An alpha.

'You're suggesting one of them was there with him?' gasps Shiner. 'On that scaffolding?'

'That w-was the only explanation.'

I struggle through the reasoning, laying out the winning combination I thought the fruit machine had turned up for me…

– That my finding that mask meant that somebody – Alpha for sure, maybe even all of the SUN crew – had been there at the school without Motto knowing.

– That they must have waited until he was at the top, then climbed up behind him and slung the ladder.

156

— And that the ski-mask must have been dropped as they ran for it.

Before I finish Shiner's shaking his head, his fists clenching in anger. 'Why? Why?'

Part of the turf-war business? Trying to make it a tougher initiation test for Motto? I hadn't known. I'd just been convinced that what had happened to Motto had been down to them.

'The p-problem was I couldn't prove it. That's why...'

Shiner finishes the sentence for me. 'Why you talked them into a raid on the sidings? Pete, whatever possessed you?'

'They hurt Motto. I wanted to get them c-caught.'

'Because you thought we weren't on to them?'

'Yes. That's why I did it. I wanted to g-get them caught. That's why I t-tried to tell you...'

It was just about eight o'clock on the Sunday evening when I rang. I did it from a call box, my fingers shaking with nerves as I punched in the number. The voice that answered was crisp and cool.

'Thank you for calling the Anti-Graffiti Unit...'

'Hello. I want to speak to Detective Inspector Tomli—' I stopped as the voice ignored me and went on talking.

'...We're sorry, but there's nobody here to take your call at present. Please leave whatever information you have. You do not have to leave your name and telephone number, but if you do it will enable us to return your call. Please speak after the tone.'

An answering machine!

It hadn't occurred to me for one minute that I'd get an answering machine. Thinking about it, though, it was obvious. It was a Sunday evening and the Anti-Graffiti Unit wasn't likely to be a twenty-four-hour a day operation.

The high-pitched tone sounded in my ear. I started speaking, even though half my mind was trying to work out what I should do.

'There's going to be a b-b-bombing raid on the Ripple Lane Sidings. Midnight t-tonight...'

I didn't bother to go on, for that's when the obvious answer came to me. I would have to go to see Shiner in person.

I'd really wanted to talk to him on the phone, not face to face. I'd reckoned either he wouldn't believe me or he'd try to talk me out of going through with it. But my mind was set. I wanted the SUN crew caught in the act. That way nobody could have any doubts. By telling Shiner what was going to happen over the phone, I'd reasoned, he'd have no option but to be there. Now I was just going to have to try to talk him into doing it.

Backing out of the phone box, I ran all the way to his house. But, when I rang at the bell, it was Lorna who answered the door.

'What do you want?'

'Your dad. I've got to t-talk to him.'

'Then you're out of luck. He's not here. He's at the hospital.'

Sitting with Motto. Of course. Mum had spoken to him

158

a few times when she'd called the hospital ward to find out if there was any change in Motto's condition.

'When will he be back?' I asked.

Lorna shrugged. 'Half eleven, probably. That's been the usual. Since it happened he's been sitting there all hours, just in case...' She paused, her lips tightening. 'Pity he didn't think of it before.'

Half eleven. That would be too late. If I waited till then I wouldn't be at the footbridge in time.

'Why should he want to talk to you, anyway?' asked Lorna.

I struggled with the words. 'B-because I've got something to tell him. Ab-ab-about M-Motto.'

She shot me a look I'd seen so often. A mix of impatience and pity, as if she was dealing with a fool. 'What about him?' she sighed.

I had no choice. I had to tell her. At that moment she was the only one who could help. I made a massive effort to control my voice.

'T-tell him about that ladder. It didn't get moved by accident. Somebody else was there. One of the S-SUN crew.'

She looked at me, disbelieving. 'You're mad. Off your head.'

'I'm not. They're g-going to bomb the Ripple Lane Sidings tonight! I'll be there with them. L-Lorna, you've got to tell your dad that!'

She looked hard at me then, as if she was trying to read

159

my mind. Slowly, she nodded. 'All right, I'll tell him.'

'He needs to have some m-men there waiting. Tell him I'm going to lead them to the N-Norfolk Road section. That's furthest away from the electrified lines. They've g-got to jump them there, before anybody gets close to a live r-rail.'

She looked as if there was more she wanted to know, but I was already backing away down the path. 'Tell him, Lorna!'

'OK, OK. I'll tell him.'

It was five minutes to midnight when I reached the footbridge. Three of them were already there, huddled in the dull circle of light thrown out by a single street lamp.

Terry Quarm – tag 'Tel'; Colin Upton – tag 'HI2U'; Aaron Byrne – tag 'ZIP'.

Each of them was in the crew uniform of black sweatshirt and baggy jeans. They had rucksacks on their backs which clinked as they moved, and the tell-tale shapes of spray cans bulged out from the double pockets along the legs of their jeans. None of them was wearing ski-masks – yet. I didn't doubt they had them tucked away somewhere, though.

They barely acknowledged me, just stayed huddled together, each trying not to show the excitement and fear churning inside.

'Wh-where are the others?' I asked.

'They'll be here,' growled Quarm. He was trying to look unconcerned but couldn't stop himself glancing in the

160

direction from which he expected them to come. Byrne and Upton did the same. The three of them looked like lost sheep.

It only confirmed what I'd worked out already. None of them was the leader of the SUN crew. It had to be one of the other two – Anstice or whoever. And whichever of that pair it was had to be 'Alpha'.

Alpha. First letter. Number one. Leader. And the owner of the ski-mask I'd found at the bottom of the scaffolding.

After a couple of minutes waiting, Quarm looked up suddenly. Two figures had just turned the corner. Immediately he, Byrne and Upton shuffled up to my shoulder.

'Told you they'd be here, didn't I?' said Quarm.

I watched the two figures approach, both unrecognisable in the shadows until Karl Anstice moved ahead and stepped into the light.

'Now!' he commanded.

Quarm instantly grabbed me from behind. As he wrenched one arm up into a hammerlock, Byrne and Upton took the other side. Between them they quickly dragged me away from the lamp and back into a dingy, paper-strewn alcove beneath the footbridge.

Anstice followed slowly, no emotion on his face, none in his voice either as he spoke.

'You're stupid, Pete. You know that? Real stupid. Even more stupid than we all thought.'

'Trying to tip off the cops,' snarled Quarm in my ear.

Anstice pushed his face closer to mine. 'That's bad news, y'know. Bad news.' He turned. 'That right?'

From behind him, the fifth figure sidled forward. 'It is for him,' said Lorna.

Karl Anstice saw the stunned look on my face and grinned. 'Hey. I reckon I should be doing the introductions. This is P-P-Pete,' he said.

Then, slipping a hand round Lorna's shoulders, he laughed softly. 'And this is Alpha.'

Chapter Seventeen

'Lorna.' Shiner says it flatly. 'So that's how they knew about the bus garage security being suspect.'

'Same way Motto did,' I say. 'By g-going through your notes without you knowing.'

Shiner looks at the loose-leaf folder, then tosses it on the table between us. 'Surprised I was there long enough for either of them to do it,' he says. 'Lorna especially. Whenever we ran into each other there was a row.'

'Motto said.'

'I didn't want her mixing with the wrong type. Went about it the wrong way, though. Just tried to make her do what I wanted, instead of taking the time to find out what she wanted.' He shakes his head and sighs. 'No wonder she went her own way. To someone she thought would put her first.'

'To Anstice.' I said.

'And she was one of them? The SUN crew?'

It shocks him as much as it had me. 'Right. She m-made that clear right away.'

Arms tightly pinned, Lorna and Karl Anstice in front of me, I struggled to take it all in.

Lorna, Motto's own sister, was one of them? Neither of us had suspected that for an instant. Why should we? It didn't make sense. She'd been the one who'd tried to warn us off, hadn't she?

Even now, seeing her in front me, close by Anstice just as I'd seen her so often in school, I could hardly believe it. Then one sudden thought crowded out everything else. If Lorna was one of them, that meant...

She might have been reading my mind. With her next breath she said, 'As you might have guessed, I didn't get round to passing your message on to my dad.'

Anstice winked, without emotion. 'She passed it on to me instead. And I passed it on to the rest of the team.'

'Grassing about tonight's action, eh?' snarled Quarm, giving my arm an extra twist to remind me he was still there.

Anstice went on. 'And lying about Motto's accident? Trying to blame it on us...'

'When all along it was your fault,' spat Lorna. 'Karl told me. None of them were anywhere near school that day.'

Anstice pushed closer, his fists tightening around the front of my jacket. 'So, Pete. What do you reckon we're going to do with you?'

He waited for the three holding me to give a little laugh, then answered his own question. 'I'll tell you. We're going on the raid, as planned. You're going to lead us into those sidings, as planned. And then we're going to tag every single one of those trains.'

'SUN crew, yeah!' hissed Byrne.

'No, man. Not this time. We're going to bomb them, all right. But this time there's only going to be one tag found on them...' He moved in close, gripping my jacket in his fists. '*Your* tag, P-P-Pete.'

There was nothing I could do to resist, and they knew it. Shouting for help wouldn't have done a thing. There weren't any houses within earshot.

As for trying to run for it – no chance. Quarm, Byrne and Upton didn't let me out of their reach. What they did do was to force me to go ahead, so that they only had to follow in my footsteps.

First, we went over the wall beneath the footbridge, dropping down the metre or so to the sloping embankment. From there it took no time at all to slide down, brushing through the overgrown grass and past the odd stunted tree, until we reached the bottom. It was like being in another world.

The footbridge and the street lamp high above us were in the world we'd just come from. They looked safe and comfortable. But in this new world all was darkness and silent danger.

Glinting in the moonlight, were the four stretches of track which ran east of the sidings: two for the main-line service and two for the underground trains. Instant death only metres away.

In the distance, I just could make out the sidings. Beyond them, casting a dull glow, were the lights of

Longbridge Station itself.

'Is this the closest we could get in?' asked Upton. He sounded nervous.

'Yes,' I said. 'It's all back g-gardens further up.'

Anstice turned me by the shoulder. 'Then you'd better get moving hadn't you? We haven't got all night.'

I started to lead them along, the shingle crunching loudly beneath our feet. My mind was a jumble of thoughts. Could I make a run for it? Little chance. To stand any hope at all I'd be better off waiting until we were actually in the sidings themselves. Then I might be able to take them by surprise, run into the floodlights and the area covered by the closed-circuit TV cameras...

The other thing I couldn't get out of my mind was the revelation that Lorna was Alpha; that the ski-mask I'd found beneath the scaffolding had got her tag on the back of it.

Anstice had said that none of them were there. Maybe he didn't know. It could just have been her: Alpha, the leader. But...Motto's own sister? Had they hated each other that much?

I heard a voice behind me, Quarm's I thought, but difficult to tell because it sounded so shaky. 'What's it like up there?' he asked.

I stopped to answer, but was pushed onwards by a rough shove in the back. 'Keep moving.'

Trudging on, I spoke over my shoulder. The words came surprisingly well.

'The underground track nearest us b-branches into

166

another six, one after another. It all happens inside a distance of about fifty m-metres.'

'How many trains on each branch?' calls Anstice.

'There's room for two on each branch. If it's not full there'll be more of them at the f-far end. They r-reverse out of the station.'

I was trying to make the far end sound more attractive, giving me less distance to cover if I made a break for it. It didn't work.

'We'll stick to this end,' says Anstice flatly.

We were getting nearer. In the distance I could make out the dull reflections of the glass in the drivers' cabs. Snaking back from them, the trains themselves blended into the darkness.

Behind me, there'd been a constant low murmur as the others had whispered and given the occasional bark of laughter. But as, ahead of us, we gradually began to get a clearer and clearer view of the single ribbon of electrified track dividing into separate silver streamers, the voices faded.

I was their prisoner, but they were starting to feel the tension too. We all knew that, any minute now, we were going to have to cross some track.

And then, suddenly, we were there. Beyond the two sets of parallels which are the up and down main lines, the first division of the electrified track was clear to see.

I stopped, and this time I wasn't pushed on again. 'Here,' I said. 'We g-go over here.'

'Why not wait till we're further up?' says Upton, his breathing audible.

'B-because it's safer. If we go across here, we can follow the right-most line all the way into the s-sidings. If we wait until we're further up it'll be like trying to cross a m-minefield.'

I turned to look at them. Anstice moved forward, gripping my wrist, Lorna sticking close to his side. The other three shuffled into position behind them.

'Let's go, then,' said Anstice. 'And no false moves.'

He was making it plain. They were still watching me. But they knew as well as I did that we'd reached the point of no return. One slip here, one piece of stupidity, and it would be death. Agonising death.

We all stepped over the two sets of main lines, their sagging power lines high above our heads. The first electrified track was right in front of us.

It was the oddest sensation. At that moment I heard Dad's voice, echoing from the past. Other kids got bedtime stories when they were young. Me, I got an explanation of how a tube train worked. Time and time again.

'Its wheels run on two rails, Peter. But the train only moves because it gets electricity from what's called the live rail. This is the rail that runs along outside the other two. The train picks up that electricity through special shoes which touch the live rail as the train goes along.'

He'd look then, and I'd realise the point of the exercise had been to drum a warning into me that I'd not forget.

'A child's shoes aren't the special sort you need, Peter. People don't have them. So they can never, never step on that live rail. Understand?'

I'd nod sleepily, and drift off to sleep. But now, as I stood within touching distance of that rail, I was more awake than I'd ever been in my life.

Slowly, I put my foot over the near rail and on to the wooden sleeper beyond it. My other foot came over to follow it. I then stepped over the centre rail, the one taking the power from the train and down to earth. In front of me, so innocent and so deadly, the other wheel rail and the live rail are no more than twenty centimetres apart. They've got to be stepped over together. It's a little hop, no more, but it seemed like the furthest distance I'd ever had to jump.

A deep breath, a leap as though I was clearing a high fence rather than a pair of rails a few centimetres off the ground, and I was over. Quickly the others did the same, gasping with relief.

From there, it was just a short distance to the nearest of the dark and deserted trains. I made to go further on, trying to get them deeper into the sidings and closer to the lights. Anstice stopped me abruptly.

'That's far enough. We'll do this one first.'

The others gathered round him, as if waiting for instructions. But why Anstice? If I'd got all the other tags allocated right then he had to be CEO. Lorna was Alpha, number one.

I found out then.

169

'OK,' hissed Anstice. A thin smile to each of them. 'Masks on. One carriage each. Chief Executive Officer says: execute your orders!'

Execute orders…CEO…Chief Executive Officer. The title given to the boss man in a company. Anstice *was* the leader.

Beside him Quarm, Upton and Byrne pulled out their ski-masks and dragged them down over their faces. Then, spray cans appearing from their pockets like guns from a holster, they scattered, hurrying along the length of the train.

I risked a glance around me. With the three of them out of the way maybe I could make a break for it…

But Anstice had come prepared for the moment. 'Lorna,' he snapped, pulling a length of rope from his own rucksack, 'Tie his hands. No' – he smirked as the thought struck him – 'his ankles.'

He forced me on to my knees and Lorna swiftly wound the rope round. Anstice bent low. 'You want to try hopping over live rails with your legs tied together, Pete? Be my guest.'

'Where do you want me, Karl?' asked Lorna.

'Stay on guard. Watch him. If he so much as moves, shout.' He moved a short distance away, towards the nearest carriage and the driver's cab. Then, looking back, he hissed one more order. 'Lorna. Mask on.'

From further down the train the eerie sounds of hissing had already begun. I watched Anstice unload the rucksack from his back and quickly whip open the top. He looked inside, feeling around. Moments later he'd dropped the rucksack down at his feet and a spray can was in his hand.

He wasn't interested in me, now, just in what he was doing. For a few seconds I watched him, twisting, turning, adding random whirls of colour and lettering, at the same time mesmerising and destructive. That's what was driving him, the destruction, just as Mum had taught me by blitzing the layout.

Still on my knees, I looked up at Lorna. 'It's stupid, Lorna. Can't you s-see that?'

'No, it's not,' she said. She glanced across towards Anstice. 'Karl took me on my first bombing raid not long after we got together. We trashed the War Memorial. Next day it was in the papers. It was brilliant. For the first time ever, I'd got some attention. I'd got a life.'

'Life? Tell that to Motto.'

At the mention of her brother's name she bent closer to me, her voice low, as if she didn't want Anstice to hear.

'I tried to warn him off, that time at the shopping arcade. But he didn't want to know, did he? Even when I saw you both at the bus depot...'

The lookout by the fence. The lookout who'd been too surprised to do her job and call out a warning.

'Near the f-fence? That was you? But – you said you were Alpha. I saw an Alpha t-tag going on one of those buses.'

'That would have been Karl. I'm usually lookout. He

171

tags for me. He cares for me.' She edged even closer, her eyes moist. 'He hit you and Mark for me. That night in the hut.'

'That – that was y-your idea?'

'I told you, I wanted to put you off. I thought having the crew jump you like that would do it.'

She'd got it all wrong, though. I knew that. Couldn't she see it?

'But it d-didn't put Motto off, did it? Only made him want it m-more. He wanted the attention, same as you. And I was ready to follow him.'

'Like a sheep!' spat Lorna. 'Just like you've always done! I didn't have a mother, I didn't have a father. With you around I didn't even have a brother!' Again she looked over at Anstice. 'Now at least I've got somebody. And I could have lost him…'

She was no longer concentrating hard enough. Moving my hands down behind my back I felt for the knot in the rope tying my ankles. As my fingers began working on it I tried to keep her talking.

'Lost him? How'd you mean?'

'After he gave you both that job to get back at Stowell, and said you could join the crew if you did it. I didn't want you in. We argued about it. I told him it was you two or me.'

It was becoming clearer. She'd heard that argument I had with Motto. I'd seen her at the window as I'd left. She'd known I wasn't going to do it. She'd known

172

she only had to stop Motto.

'So that's why you w-went to the school after him,' I said.

'Me?'

I was trying to do two things now. Even as my fingers were loosening the knot, I was trying to get at the truth about Motto as well.

'I t-told you. Somebody else was there! I know they w-were.'

'You're crazy.'

'No I'm not. I found your m-mask, Lorna. With the alpha tag.' Even as I said it, behind my back I felt the knot at my ankles fall free.

She pulled back from me, incomprehension written across her face. With fumbling fingers she reached into her own rucksack, then looked down at what she'd pulled out.

It was a ski-mask.

A ski-mask bearing the tag CEO.

Even I could see there was only one explanation. Somehow Lorna and Anstice must have got their masks mixed up after a previous raid. She'd got his mask. Which could only mean...

A look of satisfaction on his face, Anstice was moving near us, ready to hit the other side of the carriage. Anstice, who – after telling Lorna to put her mask on – had looked inside his rucksack, felt around as if looking for his own, then dropped the sack at his feet

173

without putting his own mask on.

I called out to him. 'Hey, Anstice. Where's your m-mask? Why haven't you got it on?'

Lorna answered for him, defending him, still not believing the evidence of her own eyes. 'Because I've got his, that's why.' Holding out the CEO-tagged mask, she stepped across to Anstice. 'Here. You must have mine.'

I edged myself upwards, digging my toes into the shingle. I was ready to run. Before I did, though, she had to know; she had to see the evidence for herself.

'G-give it to her then,' I shouted.

Anstice tried to bluff things out. He reached down for his rucksack, made a show of looking inside before saying, 'I must have left it behind.'

Lorna looked round, trusting him, hating me.

Then I showed her. Pulling the mask from the folds of my jacket, I held it out for her to see. 'He d-did leave it behind, Lorna. At the school, the day of Motto's accident. Here it is. I f-found it.'

She didn't have a chance to react. At that instant, a battery of lights blazed on. Blinding lights, not just at the far end of the siding where I knew they were, but very close to.

'Stay where you are, all of you,' commanded a voice, booming out through a megaphone.

All along the length of the train Quarm, Upton and Byrne froze, caught like rabbits in a car's headlights. Only Anstice reacted. Wrenching Lorna by the arm he swung her

174

round and began to run, back towards the way I'd brought them in.

Reaching the point where we'd crossed, he hesitated for a moment, then rushed forward half leading, half dragging the screaming Lorna across the electrified track and missing the live rail by a whisker...

Even as I'm telling Shiner and Mum this I pause for a moment and glance at her. It's because, from a dark corner of my mind, I find I'm asking questions of myself.

Had I thought about what I did next? Had it flashed through my mind that Lorna could get killed, that Shiner didn't deserve to lose both his children? Had it entered my head for an instant that I could get killed myself?

No. In that split second all I'd known was that I had to do my best to save Lorna, just like I'd known that I'd had no choice but to climb up that scaffolding to help Motto.

Without thinking, I'd gone after them...

I stumbled across the shingle, kicking up stones. As I got close to the junction my foot slipped, making me slither towards the live rail. It gave Anstice extra seconds to get away, to get close to the embankment I knew he was trying to reach.

Heart pounding I recovered my balance, stepped over the live rail, over the next, and started running again. They'd reached the two main lines. Lorna looked as if she was trying to hold Anstice back, but he dragged her on, picking his way carefully across the rails of the down line.

But I was sprinting now. There was nothing to hold me back. Leaping across the down line, I reached the track next to it just as they got across. A second leap and I was within touching distance.

I lunged and grabbed his jacket, pulling him backwards, stopping him from scrambling up the embankment. He lost his balance and so did I, the two of us rolling like logs down to the shingle again.

Wildly, he tried to shake me off, lashing out as though he'd got a cat clawing at him. I staggered and lost my footing, falling to my knees in a shower of gravel. Before I knew it I was on my back, my head only a whisker away from the nearest rail.

Blind with rage, he fell on top of me, pinning me down with his knees, grabbing my arms and trying to twist them above my head.

'Lorna, help me!' I yelled.

But she was just standing, transfixed, seeming not to want to go on without Anstice but unable to bring herself to help him. I had to get through to her.

'Lorna. You've got to believe me. He was there!'

As I shouted, Anstice glanced Lorna's way. It was my chance. Jerking upwards with all my strength I threw him off me, reversing our positions by rolling over and on top of him. Snatching at his arm, I pulled it back over his head and towards the rail just centimetres away.

'He was there,' I shouted. 'He d-did that ladder!'

'Don't believe him, Lorna.'

I found strength I didn't know I had. He was bucking, trying to force me off, but it wasn't working. I'd got my knees on to his chest and was bearing down on him with all my might. I pushed his hand still closer to the rail.

'Tell her!'

He knows what I'm doing and there's fear in his eyes now, real fear. 'Lorna! Stop him!' he shouts.

'Tell her!'

I'd got his hand only a couple of centimetres away from the rail now. I could keep it there or push it down at will and he knew it.

'Tell her!' I scream again.

'Yes, I did it! I ditched the ladder!'

Hearing him admit it, Lorna's eyes shut for an instant, as if she was seeing the whole of her life run through.

Anstice cried out to her. 'He was gutless, Lorna! He was scared of heights! I couldn't let someone like that join the crew! I had to test him!'

Lorna's face was like stone. She took a step forward, close to us. It was enough. I could see she knew the truth.

I was about to release Anstice's hand when she put her foot on my wrist and pressed down.

Feeling his fingers touch the cold metal of the rail, Anstice screamed...

Moments later Shiner and his men had surrounded us. As they dragged Anstice's limp body away from the track Lorna turned aside, overwhelmed by what she'd just done.

'Is…is he dead?' She nearly choked on the words.

I almost laughed. She hadn't realised. Neither of them had. I pointed up at the overhead cables, snaking high above us, exactly as Dad had built them into his layout.

'F-fainted, I reckon. This is a m-main line. The track's not electrified.'

Chapter Eighteen

'For once, being dedicated to duty worked out,' says Shiner. 'Sunday night's a popular night for tagging. I wanted to leave a few instructions for the next day, while I came back here to the hospital. So I checked the Unit's answerphone.'

'And got my m-message.'

He nods. 'And the rest, as they say, is history.'

Slowly, Shiner closes the folder on his lap and from the other side of the low coffee table he smiles at me. It's over. Now he knows the full story — mine and Motto's story. And I can tell he believes me, even before he says it:

'Thank you, Pete. Thank you.'

I look around me. It feels as if we've been in this visitors' room for hours. In that time it's as if we've been the only people in the world. Now, other sounds and sights break in: nurses hurrying to and fro; the hospital smell hanging in the air; the sign pointing down the corridor to where Motto still lies.

And again I become aware of Mum sitting beside me. She's hardly moved since I began talking, but now she puts a hand on my arm.

'Do you want to go home?'

'Can I see M-Motto first?'

The three of us make our way down the corridor and into the small ward where Motto's bed is. His eyes are closed and his face looks as if the life has been drained from it – as if he's an android now, instead of a commander.

Lorna is sitting there with him, next to her mother. Shiner goes round to sit between them, taking one of their hands in each of his. The family of Motto's dreams, and he can't see it – yet.

'How is he?' I ask.

Motto's mum glances at Shiner, then up at me. 'He's a bit better, Pete. The doctors say there are signs that he's coming out of the coma. He's starting to wake up.'

She looks like she's going to say more, then chokes. It's Shiner that says it for her.

'They also say his brain might be a bit damaged. Not seriously, but – it could show.'

'He...' says Motto's mum slowly, as if she's remembering a day long past, 'he might not be as clever as he was. Do you understand?'

I do understand. She's saying that when he wakes up we could be equals. Androids together. I don't know if I'll be able to handle that. Not so long ago I definitely wouldn't, but now – maybe. But then again, maybe it won't come to that.

Still, I nod, and say, 'Yes. Yes, I understand.'

Lorna reaches for her mum's hand, but she's looking at me. 'Mark's going to be OK, Mum. He's got us to help him. All of us.'

*

I don't talk much on the way home because I'm thinking, testing some answers – answers I've come up with to the questions I'd found myself asking as I told them about what happened in the sidings.

Finally, I know I've got to test them on the one person who can tell me if I've got it right or wrong.

'Mum. You know when I went after Anstice...' I begin.

She nods but says nothing, just lets me carry on in my own time.

'I didn't think about the danger. It was the same when I went up on that scaffolding after Motto. I didn't think about the danger then, either. I didn't think about me.' I turn to look at her, hoping she knows how much she means to me. 'I didn't think about you.'

I reckons she senses what's going through my mind even before I do, but still she says nothing.

'That...that's how it was with Dad, wasn't it? When he died?'

Now she speaks, softly.

'Yes, Peter. I'm sure that's how it was. When he saw that train bearing down on him, he didn't have time to think. He could only do what his heart told him to do.'

'Stick with it. Do his best to prevent a crash. Save the people on that train.'

'And it cost him his life. He died because he was thinking of them...'

'Not because he'd forgotten about me. Right?'

181

She looks at me then, and in her eyes it's like her prayer's been answered. 'Right,' she says.

It's like a massive cloud has cleared, and I'm still in a daze as we reach home. So it's only as I'm walking to the front door that I realise I'm on my own. Mum's gone briskly down the side of the house and is unlocking the garage door.

Inside, after what I've just come to understand, I can hardly bring myself to look at the paint-splattered layout Dad put that same heart into making. But Mum's already taking her coat off and studying it keenly.

'We can have all this cleaned off in a couple of weeks, you know.' She catches my look of amazement. 'I mean it. A bit of elbow grease, that's all it'll take. It's not as if I haven't cleaned off graffiti before!'

She's going round the trestle table, pointing out the damage to the different parts. 'That's not as bad as it looks. That won't take much doing…'

Suddenly she stops. One small figure has miraculously escaped the blitz. She picks it up. It's one of the dozens of railway workers that Dad made and scattered around various places in the layout.

'Well, will you look at that! Is that your dad, or isn't it?'

Powerful. Stocky. Dressed in a driver's uniform. I can see what she means. The little figure does remind me of him, as if Dad was playing a little private joke when he made it.

Except that it's a joke that doesn't make me laugh. The

words fall out, just as they have before. 'I miss him, Mum. I still miss him. I wish so much he was still here.'

'Oh, Peter. He is here.'

For a moment I think Mum's making a bad joke herself, talking about the little figure.

But she's not. I can see that from the way she's looking at me.

'I mean it. He is here. I can see him, even if you can't. I see him every day.' She sighs. 'I see him whenever I look at you.'

As she moves to my side. I realise for the first time that I'm now taller than she is.

'I hear him when you speak,' she says. 'I see him when you smile. I feel him when you're near. Oh, Peter, take a good look in a mirror. You're your father's son.'

She reaches up and puts her hands on my shoulders. 'Don't you see, love? Don't you understand? Your dad's still alive. He's living through you.'

In that moment I do see. I do understand.

And so I do the only thing I can that will really prove it to her. Unpinning the wrinkled, yellowed newspaper photograph from the notice board, I tear it into little pieces.

Then I talk.

About Dad.

About what's to come – the court cases and how I'll have to take whatever they bring.

About Motto, my friend Motto, and what we'll do when

he's up and about again. About how he's going to need me to help him, show him around, teach him things.

I talk and I talk.

And it's a good while before I realise that since we left the hospital I haven't stuttered once.

**More Black Apples
to get your teeth into...**

Also by **Michael Coleman**

'You scared Daniel?'

How many times has Tozer said that to me? Hundreds.

But this time it's different. We're not in school. He hasn't got me in a headlock, with one of his powerful fists wrenching my arm up, asking 'You scared, Weirdo?'

No. We're here, trapped underground together with no way out.

Shortlisted for the Carnegie Medal,
Lancashire Children's Book Award and Writers Guild Award.
'Tense and psychological.' *The Times*

1 84362 299 8   £4.99

Luke is a thief who knows that crime *does* pay. Besides, what other way is there for someone like him?

Then he meets Jodi. She might be blind, but she can see where Luke's life is going wrong. And she has a burning ambition that only Luke can help her fulfil...if she can trust him.

So Luke decides to go straight. But when old acquaintances want to use his talents for one last job, can he resist? Or will he end up on the run again?

£4.99

1 84121 161 3

Ever heard of a Readathon? Well, Robbie and his mates have come up with something much more exciting: a snogathon! But it's top secret. Imagine how the girls would feel to know they're being ranked by snogabillity!

Robbie wants to win the competition by snogging Mel, the ice maiden. But Mel might just have other ideas...

'A very readable and amusing book. A story remarkable for its insights and full of funny incidents. This is a very entertaining and positive novel that will be devoured.'
The School Librarian

Bernard Ashley

1 86039 879 0   £4.99

When Kaninda survives a brutal attack on his village in East Africa he joins the rebel army, where he's trained to carry weapons, and use them. But then aid workers take him to London. Clan and tribal conflicts are everywhere, and on the streets it's estate versus estate, urban tribe against urban tribe.

All Kaninda wants is to get back to his own war. But together with Laura Rose, the daughter of his new family, he is drawn into a dangerous local conflict that is spiralling out of control.

**Shortlisted for the Carnegie Medal
and the *Guardian* Children's Fiction Award**

'So pacy that it is difficult to turn the pages fast enough.'
The School Librarian

'Compelling and unforgettable.' *Time Out*

1 84121 814 6   £4.99

Marsh End. Lonely, isolated and bleak, Sophia's mum loves it. But for Sophia, the brooding skies hold no solace for her lost father, or her lost life in London. Nothing ever happens in this dead end place.

That is until Revenge House begins to reveal its murky secrets, and Sophia and her mum find themselves sucked into a brutal criminal underworld that will eventually threaten their lives.

Shortlisted for the *Guardian* Children's Fiction Award

'Briskly streetwise with a dramatic, uncontrived conclusion.'
Times Educational Supplement

'A tense, classy thriller. Ashley sets a tone and style that is very contemporary and will have wide appeal.'
Books for Keeps

More Orchard Black Apples

☐ **Going Straight**	*Michael Coleman*	1 84362 299 8
☐ **The Snog Log**	*Michael Coleman*	1 84121 161 3
☐ **Tag**	*Michael Coleman*	1 84362 182 7
☐ **Weirdo's War**	*Michael Coleman*	1 84362 183 5
☐ **Little Soldier**	*Bernard Ashley*	1 86039 879 0
☐ **Revenge House**	*Bernard Ashley*	1 84121 814 6
☐ **Horowitz Horror**	*Anthony Horowitz*	1 84121 455 8
☐ **More Horowitz Horror**	*Anthony Horowitz*	1 84121 607 0
☐ **The Mighty Crashman**	*Jerry Spinelli*	1 84121 222 9
☐ **Stargirl**	*Jerry Spinelli*	1 84121 926 6
☐ **Get a Life**	*Jean Ure*	1 84121 831 6

All priced at £4.99

Orchard Black Apples are available from all good bookshops,
or can be ordered direct from the publisher:
Orchard Books, PO BOX 29, Douglas IM99 1BQ
Credit card orders: please telephone 01624 836000 or fax 01624 837033
or visit our Internet site: www.wattspub.co.uk
or e-mail: bookshop@enterprise.net for details.

To order please quote title, author and ISBN
and your full name and address.
Cheques and postal orders should be made payable to 'Bookpost plc.'
Postage and packing is FREE within the UK
(overseas customers should add £1.00 per book).
Prices and availability are subject to change.